Puffin Books

Midnite

One morning His Honour Justice Pepper put on
his long curly wig and his long robes and got into a
mail-coach. There was another person on the coach with
him, and his name was Trooper O'Grady.

When they were about twenty miles from the town
and were going up a very steep hill, a voice called
out, 'Stand and deliver! Your money or your
lives.' Then there was a thunderous crash, and out of
the thick bush bounded a tall and noble-minded
horse, with a long-legged bushranger on his back.
(A bushranger is the name for an Australian
highwayman.)

'Your money or your life?' asked the bushranger.

'Oh, my money,' said the Judge, shaking from head
to foot, 'of course,' and he pulled out his fat purse
and his watch, and gave them to the bushranger.

That was the very first meeting between the terrifying
(but rather stupid) Captain Midnite and his best
human friend, Trooper O'Grady; and which was the
most wicked who can say? – for strangely enough
the Judge's possessions ended up in Trooper's pockets,
and he forgot to mention this to the Judge.

Anyone from eight upwards will enjoy this brilliantly
good-humoured and amusing history of the exploits
of Captain Midnite and his five good animal
friends.

Randolph Stow

Midnite

*The Story of a Wild
Colonial Boy*

Illustrated by
Ralph Steadman

Puffin Books

Penguin Books Australia Ltd,
487 Maroondah Highway, P.O. Box 257
Ringwood, Victoria 3134, Australia
Penguin Books Ltd,
Harmondsworth, Middlesex, England
Viking Penguin Inc.
40 West 23rd Street, New York, N.Y. 10010, U.S.A.
Penguin Books Canada Limited,
2801 John Street, Markham, Ontario, Canada
Penguin Books (N.Z.) Ltd,
182–190 Wairau Road, Auckland 10, New Zealand

First published by Macdonald 1967
First published by Puffin Books 1969
Reprinted 1976, 1977, 1978, 1980, 1982 (twice), 1983 (twice), 1985,
1986 (twice), 1987

Printed in Australia by
Australian Print Group, Maryborough, Vic.
Set in Linotype Pilgrim

CIP

Stow, Randolph, 1935–
Midnite

(Puffin Books)
For children.
ISBN 0 14 030421 5

I. Title. (Series).

A823'.3

To the wild Colonial memory of
Moondyne Joe
Bushranger, Escapologist, Nostrum-monger and
Captain Starlight
Bushranger, Gentleman, Clerk of the Geological Survey
Department, W.A.

Acknowledgement

The Song
Yes! Let Me Like A Soldier Fall
is by Mr W. V. Wallace of the 19th Century

Contents

1

Captain Midnite's Gang

Once upon a time, in Western Australia a hundred years ago, a young man lived with his father in a cottage in a forest. The young man was called Midnite. At least, that is what I am going to call him, because that is what he called himself, later on, when he was famous. I am not going to put his real name into a book, because there are some people in Australia who might not like it.

The cottage was very small, with a roof made of bark and a verandah all around it. It stood on the slope of a valley, in the middle of an orchard, which was all pink-and-white with fruit blossom in the spring, and all shiny green-and-gold with orange and lemon trees summer and winter. At the bottom of the valley was a pretty creek, running through bracken and wild palms. Except for the orchard, and the paddocks where the horse and cow lived, there was nothing around Midnite's house except tall forest.

Midnite's mother had died when he was quite young, and he and his father lived all alone. His father had once been a sea-captain, and had brought home lots of shells and coral and carved boxes and little elephants and that sort of thing, as well as a very wise and handsome Siamese cat called Khat. Khat had blue eyes and mostly cream-coloured fur, with a coffee-coloured tail, and a coffee-coloured mask on his face, a bit like a bank-robber.

Besides Khat, there were four other animals living with Midnite and his father. There was a rather silly cow called Dora, who was not nearly so young as she thought she was. There was a very tall and noble-minded horse called Red Ned, with a strawberry-coloured body and a pale mane and tail. There was a cockatoo called Major, because he was a Major Mitchell cockatoo, which is hard to describe to anyone who has not seen a Major Mitchell cockatoo, but if you have seen what the clouds look like when the sun is coming up, then you can imagine the colour of Major's best feathers. Last of all, there was a young sheepdog called Gyp, who was always laughing and frowning at the same time, because he was never sure whether he was doing the right thing.

One day Midnite's father became ill, and soon afterwards he died. It is sad to have to begin a story like this, but that is what happened and this is a true book. So Midnite was left alone in the world with his five animals.

This made him very sorry and lonely, and for a long time he did nothing except sit on the verandah all day, whittling sticks with his pocket-knife and thinking sad thoughts. Sometimes a tear ran down his cheek, and when the young sheepdog, Gyp, saw this, he cried out loud. Day after day Midnite sat there, whittling sticks and forgetting to cook his dinner.

One day a voice said to him: 'Don't you think it is dinner-time?'

'I'm not hungry,' said Midnite.

'Aren't you?' said the voice. 'I am.'

Midnite went on whittling as if he had not heard, but after a while he began to wonder who it was who had spoken to him, for he was sure that he had never known anyone with a Siamese accent. He looked round at Khat, who was sitting beside him.

'Did you speak to me?' Midnite asked.

'I did,' said Khat.

'I didn't know you could talk,' said Midnite. 'You have never talked before.'

'There was nothing to talk about,' said Khat, yawning.

'How peculiar,' said Midnite; and he went on whittling, frowning with thought.

This is the place to tell you some things about Midnite that make him different from most heroes in books. One of these things you may have guessed already. It is that Midnite was not very clever. In fact, he was rather stupid, though even Khat forgave him this, because he was so good-natured. Another thing is that he was not very handsome, not nearly so handsome as Khat or Major or Red Ned, and he always needed a haircut. But he had nice blue eyes, white teeth, and a brown smiling face. It is hard to decide whether to call him a young man or a boy, and he was not sure himself which he was, but he thought that he was probably a young man. He was seventeen, and had begun to use his father's razor, though to tell the truth he had hardly any whiskers to shave off with it, and Khat used to laugh at him when he pretended. Khat was a rather superior person, and had splendid whiskers.

Well, Midnite went on whittling and thinking, and Khat went on looking at him. After a while, Khat said: 'You are sad.'

'Yes,' said Midnite. 'I am sad because I have no father and no money and nothing in the world except this house and this orchard.'

'And me,' said Khat.

'And you, of course,' said Midnite.

'Let us have dinner,' said Khat, 'and then we will talk about money.'

So Midnite went into the kitchen and cooked the dinner, and they ate it on the verandah, so that Gyp and Major and Red Ned and Dora could listen to the conversation.

'Now,' said Khat, when he had finished his dinner and was enjoying a saucer of tea, 'What are your plans?'

'I have no plans,' said Midnite, looking sad.

'If I were you,' said Khat, 'I should be a bushranger.'

'Would you, really?' said Midnite.

'I should call myself Captain Midnight,' said Khat, 'which is a fine name for a bushranger, but I should spell it M-I-D-N-I-T-E.'

'Why?' asked Midnite.

'Because that is more fierce and romantic,' said Khat. 'There is nothing romantic about good spelling.'

'Well,' said Midnite, 'that is an interesting plan, but what does a bushranger do?'

'He bushranges horses and cattle and sheep,' said Khat, 'and he holds up people's coaches and takes their money and their watches. Or their lives,' Khat added, 'but money and watches are more usual.'

'If I bushrange horses and cattle and sheep,' said Midnite, 'where am I to put them? People would come looking for them.'

'You must have a Secret Hideout,' said Khat, 'and I know the very place.'

'Oh,' said Midnite, 'do you mean the Hidden Valley?'

'Of course,' said Khat. 'Nobody knows how to find it except us.'

'That is a *very* interesting plan,' said Midnite, looking much happier. 'When shall we start being bushrangers?'

'Why not tomorrow?' said Khat. 'We can take all the pots and pans and things that we need, and we can live in the caves of the Hidden Valley quite comfortably.'

'Khat,' said Midnite, 'you are a very wise and handsome cat, and you can sleep in my bed for ever after, so long as you don't wash your face all night.'

'Thank you,' said Khat. 'That is exactly what I was going to do.'

The next day Midnite saddled Red Ned, and tied the pots and pans and food and blankets to the saddle, and they all set off for the Hidden Valley. Dora went first, and she was even sillier than usual, jumping around and running off into the bush and hiding, so that everyone got quite annoyed with her, and Gyp nipped her heels, and Major, who had a very bad temper sometimes, flew down and nipped her ear. In this fashion, chasing and scolding Dora all the way, they arrived at the Hidden Valley.

The Valley was like a great big paddock, and was a very secret place indeed. The steep rocky hills closed it in on three sides, and on the fourth side was a river, with red cliffs on the far bank of it. They were not cliffs of rock, but cliffs of red earth, and they looked very pretty when the sun shone on them. The only way into the Valley was through a gap in the hills so narrow that it only needed a gate across it to shut in the Valley completely and make it like a fenced field. In the side of the hills were big caves with rather clever paintings on the walls, made by the black people long ago. When Midnite had come to the biggest and most comfortable of these caves, Khat said: 'Let us stop here, and make this cave our Hideout.'

'Very well,' said Midnite. And before long they had turned the cave into quite a nice sort of house.

'Now,' said Khat, 'you must make a gate across the track into the Hidden Valley, so that when we have bushranged our horses and cattle and sheep they will not be able to get out again.'

All day Midnite laboured, building the gate, and when the sun was setting and the grass was glowing very green and the cliffs across the river were glowing very red, the gate was finished.

'Leave it open,' said Khat, 'and come back to the cave, and let us have supper.'

While they were having supper, Midnite noticed that Red

Ned and Gyp and Major and Dora had all disappeared. 'Where have they gone?' he asked Khat.

'They are preparing a surprise for you,' said Khat. 'Don't ask questions, but clean your teeth and go to bed, and in the morning you will be most astonished.'

Midnite was a bit annoyed at being told to clean his teeth by a cat, but he did it, and went to bed, and was soon fast asleep. In the morning, he was awakened by a voice whispering: 'Captain Midnite' in his ear.

'What is it?' Midnite asked, sleepily, when he had opened his eyes and seen that it was Khat who was whispering.

'Get up and close the gate,' said Khat. 'The surprise is here.'

Midnite got up, rubbing his eyes, and walked out of the cave, and then he certainly was most astonished. There was a white mist rising from the grass and the river, and in the mist he saw thirteen horses and thirty-one head of cattle and seventy-six sheep.

'Where did they come from?' Midnite asked, staring.

'Go and close the gate,' said Khat, 'and I will explain to you on the way.'

This is what Khat told Midnite as they walked through the wet grass.

First of all, he told him about Dora. The thing to remember about Dora is that she was an extremely aggravating cow, and she knew it. She was a big old yellow cow with hips like a garden gate, and a queer sense of humour. When Dora went out to bushrange cattle for Midnite, this is how she did it.

She went to where she knew the cattle were, and waited quite a long way from them, until she knew that they had seen her. Then she started jumping around and chasing her tail and behaving in the silliest way, all the while pretending that she didn't know that they knew that she knew that they were watching. She pretended that she was having a

15

great old time all by herself, which is a very aggravating sort of showing-off, just as aggravating when a cow does it as when a little girl does it. After a while all the cattle started murmuring to each other. At first they murmured that it was sad to see the poor silly thing carrying on like that at her age. But as Dora only went on getting sillier and more aggravating, they began to murmur: 'Let's rush up and butt her in the ribs.' Soon they started to galumph towards her, and when they came near, Dora galumphed off into the bush. They galumphed for miles and miles and miles, and whenever the cattle lost sight of Dora, she waited for them, and then jumped out of the bush and aggravated them again. The cattle became so angry that they hardly knew where they were going, and at last they chased Dora right through the open gate into the Hidden Valley.

As soon as they were safe inside, Dora went and hid in one of the caves, and the cattle settled down to eating the grass and forgot about her.

Next, Khat told Midnight about Red Ned. The thing to remember about Red Ned is that he was a very tall and noble-minded horse, and when he went out to bushrange horses for Midnite, he did it in quite a different way from Dora. He went to the place where he knew the horses were, and he just stood there, looking noble. After a while all the horses were so impressed and so curious that they couldn't eat or do anything except stare at Red Ned and wonder who he was. Bit by bit they began to come closer to him, and as soon as they did, Red Ned walked on. They followed and he walked, he walked and they followed, until at last they came through the open gate into the Hidden Valley. Then Red Ned allowed them to catch up with him, and when they stood around him, feeling shy, he said a few noble-minded things to them, and they decided to stay in the Hidden Valley for ever after.

Thirdly, Khat told Midnite about Gyp. The thing to remember about Gyp is that he was always frowning and
smiling at the same time, and looking worried and wondering whether he was doing the right thing. He looked like
this because he was a sheepdog. All sheepdogs have this
look, and if you have ever seen a dog rounding up one sheep
or two sheep, you will know why. It is easier for a dog to
drive one or two lions than one or two sheep, because at
least lions have brains and some idea of where they want
to go. A sheep is the stupidest animal in the world, and
hardly an animal at all, but more like a sort of walking
cotton-bush. However, when Gyp went to bushrange sheep
for Midnite, he bushranged seventy-six of them and it is
much easier to drive seventy-six sheep than one or two.
So he was able to bring them into the Hidden Valley without
too much trouble, though of course, being sheep, they
jumped over invisible objects all the way, and behaved very
childishly.

All these things Khat explained to Midnite while they
were walking to the gate and closing it. As they were
going back to the cave, a fat white duck and twelve
yellow ducklings came out of the grass and ran away from
them.

'I have been busy making plans for the others,' said Khat
modestly, 'and I have only had time to bushrange one duck
and her ducklings.'

'Oh,' said Midnite, in a thoughtful voice. 'So everybody
has been busy, except Major and me.'

When Major heard Midnite say that, the crest on his head
stood up with rage, and he screamed. The thing to remember about Major is that he was always flying into terrible rages. Perhaps he knew that when he was bad-tempered
he looked extremely handsome; for when his crest was
standing up and his wings were flapping, he showed all his
most beautiful feathers.

'Major has been busy, too,' said Khat; and he led Midnite to the box where Major had hidden all the things that he had bushranged. In the box were rings and watches and brooches and a silver christening mug and a great deal of money, as well as a few things that Major had bushranged for himself, such as buttons and clothes-pegs and a piece of mirror and a picture of Queen Victoria in five colours.

'I am sorry, Major,' said Midnite. 'You have worked very hard.'

After making this apology, Midnite sat down in front of the cave and began to whittle a stick, with his hair falling in his eyes.

'You are sad,' said Khat.

'Not very,' said Midnite. 'Just a little.'

'You ought not to be sad,' said Khat. 'You are a most successful bushranger.'

'Yes,' said Midnite, 'but I have done nothing myself. It has all been done for me.'

Khat sat and thought, and after a while he began to purr.

'What have you thought of?' asked Midnite.

'We will hold up a coach,' said Khat, 'and rob the passengers, and that will make you famous.'

'Will they write about me in the newspapers?' Midnite wondered.

'I should think they would,' said Khat. 'I should think they would make up songs about you, too. People are always making up songs about bushrangers.'

'Perhaps they will put me into a book,' said Midnite, growing excited.

'I should not be surprised,' said Khat, turning his wise blue eyes into wise blue slits as he tried to look into the future. 'I think I see somebody, a hundred years from today, sitting at a typewriter, making up a book called *Midnite*.'

18

'What is a typewriter?' asked Midnite.

'It is a machine for writing books,' said Khat. 'People living a hundred years from today will be preposterously lazy.'

2

Captain Midnite Strikes

One morning His Honour Mr Justice Pepper (or Judge Pepper as he was called for short) put on his long curly wig made of horse-hair and his long robes, and packed his little hammer in a little suitcase, and got into a mail-coach. Judge Pepper's job was to send people like bushrangers to the great grey gaol by the sea, and the hammer was for banging on his Bench with to stop people from laughing in Court. Judge Pepper was a fat red-faced shiny man with a fat shiny watch and chain. He was very bad-tempered, and he was going in the coach to a country town to sentence a few people to spend years and years in prison.

There was another person in the coach with Judge Pepper, and his name was Trooper O'Grady. It is not easy to describe Trooper O'Grady. He was a rather tall thin man with the sort of face that got lines on it when he laughed, and he laughed a lot. He was a very popular man, and even Judge Pepper didn't hate him, although he was quite young for a grown-up, only twenty-four, and Judge Pepper usually did hate young people. Judge Pepper said that he was very polite, which was true; but there were other things about Trooper O'Grady that the Judge had not thought of. A trooper is a kind of policeman who usually rides a horse, and what the Judge had never considered is that a policeman, who is always mixing with people who steal and that sort of thing, might come to learn bad habits from them. There was another thing, too, that the Judge had never considered, and that is that a young man who had already learned bad habits might feel safer if he became a policeman.

The coach rattled away through the town, and over a bridge, and was soon in the country. Birds were singing, and the bush was full of flowers, and even Judge Pepper was quite pleased to be going on a journey in such splendid weather. He made a joke now and then, and Trooper O'Grady laughed heartily, which showed what a polite young man he was. When they came to the hills, Trooper O'Grady got out and walked to make the coach lighter for the horses. As he walked along, he talked and made jokes with the driver, and the driver said to himself: 'What a nice chap.'

When they were about twenty miles from the town, and were going up a very steep hill, a voice called out of the bush: 'Stand and deliver! Your money or your lives!'

'Who said that?' demanded the Judge, sticking his red face out of the coach window.

'A bushranger, Your Honour,' said Trooper O'Grady. 'That is what they always say.'

'Well, shoot him,' said the Judge, crossly.

'You shoot him, sir,' said the trooper. 'My pistols are inside the coach with you.'

'Throw the pistols to me,' snarled the voice in the bush, 'or you are a dead man.'

'That's curious,' murmured Trooper O'Grady. 'The voice has a Siamese accent.'

'Don't make personal remarks,' snapped Khat (for of course it was Khat). 'Stand with your hands above your heads, and if I catch anyone not shivering in his shoes, he's in trouble.'

Trooper O'Grady and the driver put up their hands, while

21

Judge Pepper still stared from the coach. From being a red-faced shiny man he had turned into a white-faced shiny man.

'Throw me the pistols, Judge Pepper,' called Khat, 'or I'll tear out your heart and eat it.'

'No, no,' cried Judge Pepper, trembling, as he threw the pistols into the bush. 'Have pity on me. I have a great-aunt and eleven cousins in Wagga Wagga.'

'Let them beware,' said Khat, with a bloodcurdling laugh. 'Now, Judge Pepper, get out of the coach, and stand beside Trooper O'Grady with your hands up.'

The Judge got out as he was told, though his knees were shaking so much that he could hardly walk, and he stood in a line with Trooper O'Grady and the driver.

'Our leader is coming to rob you,' said Khat. 'If any one of you moves, he is a dead man.'

'You've already said that,' remarked Trooper O'Grady.

'Keep a civil tongue in your head, O'Grady,' snarled Khat, 'or I will nail it to a tree.'

Suddenly there was a thunderous crash, and out of the thick bush bounded a tall and noble-minded horse, with a long-legged bushranger on his back. The bushranger dismounted, and strode towards Judge Pepper. He had a red handkerchief over his face, hiding everything except his blue eyes, and he held one of Trooper O'Grady's pistols in his right hand.

'Your money or your life?' he asked Judge Pepper, rather shyly.

'Oh, my money,' said the Judge, shaking from head to foot, 'of course.'

'Give me your purse, then,' said the bushranger.

'And your watch and chain,' called Khat from the bush.

'And your watch and chain,' repeated the bushranger, going red in the tops of his ears.

The Judge pulled out his fat purse and his watch, and

gave them to the bushranger, who put them carefully in the pocket of his coat.

The driver, meanwhile, had been counting the loose change that he kept in his trousers pocket, and he said to the bushranger: 'Four and twopence. Is that any use to you, mate?'

'Oh, no,' said the bushranger, embarrassed. 'No, you keep it.'

'You can have it, mate,' said the driver, 'if you need it.'

'Oh no, please,' said the bushranger, 'you have it. I've got rather a lot of money, as a matter of fact.'

'I wouldn't want to leave you short,' said the driver.

'Hold your tongue,' Khat called to the driver, 'or we'll cut your head off and send it to your mother.'

'If that's the way you feel about it, mate,' said the driver, shrugging his shoulders.

'Your Siamese confederate is very fierce,' remarked Trooper O'Grady.

'Oh, he's not, really,' said the bushranger. 'He's rather warm and cuddly, usually.'

'Are there many foreigners in your gang?' asked the trooper.

'There are seventy-two of us,' Khat called out, 'and we come from all the countries of the world.'

'And you are the leader?' said Trooper O'Grady to the bushranger. 'May I ask your name, so that I can tell the newspapers?'

'Certainly,' said the bushranger. 'My name is Captain Midnite.'

'What a dreadful name,' said the Judge, with a shiver of terror.

'Do you think so?' said Midnite. 'Truly?'

'You are rather young to be a bushranger,' observed Trooper O'Grady.

'I'm seventeen,' said Midnite, modestly.

'Seventeen!' said the trooper. 'That is most amazing. You will go far.'

'Too far for you to find me,' vaunted Midnite.

Trooper O'Grady laughed aloud, crinkling up his face. 'What a chap you are,' he said, admiringly.

Midnite blushed under his handkerchief, he was so pleased. In all his life he had never had any human friend except his father, and suddenly he felt lonely. He felt lonely because Trooper O'Grady was such a nice chap, and just the sort of person Midnite would have liked for his best friend. 'I'm pretty desperate,' he boasted, going red again in the tops of his ears.

'I'm a plain man,' said Trooper O'Grady, 'and when I like someone, I say so. You're an upstanding manly young fellow, Midnite, and I like you.'

'That's awfully good of you,' said Midnite, blushing more and more. 'Do you know, there's something about your face that made me think, as soon as I saw it: "What a nice chap".'

'That was a generous and manly thought,' said Trooper O'Grady, pleasantly, 'and does great credit to your good-nature. Which makes me think – now, I wonder – before you go (I shan't keep you a minute) will you let me whisper something, as man to man and friend to friend, in your ear? It's a word of advice,' explained the trooper, dropping his voice, 'that I wouldn't wish the Judge to hear.'

'Yes?' said Midnite, coming close.

The trooper bent his head and whispered in Midnite's ear. At the same time he put his arm around Midnite, in the friendliest way.

'O'Grady!' Khat called suddenly from the bush. 'Stand back and put up your hands, or I'll shoot you so full of holes that you will look like lace.'

'Well said,' applauded Trooper O'Grady, as he jumped back into line.

'Captain Midnite, sir,' Khat called, 'it's time to go.'

'Oh, must I?' said Midnite.

'Hurry, hurry!' called Khat, bad-temperedly. 'We shall be late for all our bank-robberies.'

'Well,' said Midnite, shyly, holding out his hand to Trooper O'Grady, 'I'm most awfully pleased to have met you.'

'Captain Midnite, I'm proud to know *you*,' said Trooper O'Grady, shaking hands and smiling his nicest smile.

Midnite bowed to the judge, and in one leap sprang to the saddle. 'Good-bye,' he cried, waving his hat to the trooper; and with that he pranced away into the bush, looking extremely bold and dashing.

'What a vile desperado,' snarled Judge Pepper, gnashing his false teeth and shaking his fist after Midnite.

'What a charming idiot,' murmured Trooper O'Grady, smiling and smiling.

Red Ned galloped and pranced and pranced and galloped until he reached the secret rendezvous where they were to meet Khat and Gyp and Major. There Midnite dismounted, and lay down to wait in the warm soft grass.

When Khat arrived, he was so angry that he looked a different cat. His coffee-coloured tail was lashing back and forth like a whip, and his blue eyes were round and glaring.

'What's the matter, Khat?' asked Midnite, in a nervous voice.

'*You* are the matter,' said Khat furiously. 'You have no more sense than – than *Dora*.'

'But what have I done?' asked Midnite.

'Why didn't you rob O'Grady?' Khat demanded.

'He was such a nice chap,' said Midnite.

'And you let him put his arm around you,' Khat cried. 'In another second, if I had not called out, he would have seized the pistol and arrested you.'

'Khat, you don't know what a nice fellow he is,' said Midnite. 'He was giving me some advice.'

'What advice?' asked Khat, scornfully.

'He said: "Beware of pickpockets".'

'*What?*' cried Khat.

' "Beware of pickpockets",' Midnite repeated. 'That's what he said.'

Khat was quiet for a long time. He closed his eyes and sat perfectly still. He held his breath and counted silently to a hundred. Then he said, softly: 'Midnite.'

'Yes?' said Midnite.

'When you robbed the Judge,' Khat said, 'you put the watch and purse into your coat pocket, did you not?'

'Yes,' said Midnite.

'Are they there now?' asked Khat.

Midnite felt in his pocket. Then he held it open and looked into it. Then he looked at Gyp, and Major, and Red Ned. Finally, he looked at Khat.

'No,' said Midnite.

Khat said nothing at all, but curled up in the grass and pretended to go to sleep.

'Khat, he *seemed* such a nice chap,' cried Midnite.

'He is a common thief,' murmured Khat, 'a common pickpocket. And you, a bushranger, have let him pick *your* pocket.'

'I shall never trust a human being again,' said Midnite, sadly.

'Don't,' advised Khat, 'and thank heaven in your prayers every night that you have five animals to look after you.'

For a long time after he was robbed by the trooper, Midnite stayed in the Hidden Valley, thinking bitter thoughts about human beings. He was so bitter that he did not want to see any human beings ever again, not even to rob them.

One day Khat said to him: 'You have not been bushranging for nearly two weeks.'

'I am too bitter,' said Midnite.

'Well, don't sit here sulking,' said Khat. 'Go out and take your revenge on the human race.'

'How?' asked Midnite.

'By robbing them,' said Khat. 'How else?'

So Midnite began bushranging again, and soon he was the terror of Australia. He held up coaches, and he bushranged sheep and horses and cattle. His name was in newspapers all over the world, and troopers and soldiers and black trackers roamed everywhere looking for him. The black trackers were Australian aborigines, who are very clever at following people's footprints in the dust, and can even tell you whose footprints they are, if it is someone they already know. But though they searched everywhere for Midnite's footprints, they never found a sign of him. This was because Khat, who was by far the wisest person in Australia, had told Midnite to make himself shoes of sheepskin, with the wool on the outside; and so the only tracks that Midnite left in the dust were little curly lines that might have been made by the wind.

Time went by, and Midnite grew more and more famous. Judges and troopers were furious with him, ladies were falling in love with him, poets were making up songs about him, and painters were painting pictures of him holding up coaches, with titles like *Bailed Up*. All the Irish people said that he was Irish, and all the English people said that he was French. The Governor's lady said that she believed that Midnite was a Duke in disguise, and the President of America said that he knew for a fact that Midnite was a down-trodden peasant spreading his eagle wings.

Here is a story to show you how famous Midnite was. One day, in the Hidden Valley, Khat said to Midnite: 'There is no more jam.'

'The best jam in the Colony is made by Mrs Chiffle,' said Midnite. 'I shall go to her house and bushrange some.'

That night he rode to Mrs Chiffle's gate, and left Red Ned in the bush. He crept up like a shadow, in his sheepskin shoes, and forced the lock of the pantry door. The house was dark, and Mrs Chiffle, who was a widow and lived all alone, was in bed. Midnite struck a match, and began to pack Mrs Chiffle's jam into his saddlebag.

'Psst!' whispered Khat, who was keeping watch. 'Someone is coming with a candle.'

In a flash, Khat had hidden himself. But it was too late for Midnite. He had only time to pull up his handkerchief over his face before Mrs Chiffle came in with a light.

Mrs Chiffle looked at Midnite's handkerchief and his sheepskin shoes, and she knew straightaway who he was. But instead of screaming, she said: 'Captain Midnite?'

'Ma'am,' said Midnite, bowing politely.

'Quick,' said Mrs Chiffle, 'hide under my bed. There is not a moment to lose. The troopers are coming.'

She ran into her bedroom, and Midnite ran after her, and slipped swift as a snake under the bed. Then Mrs Chiffle got between the sheets, and blew out the candle, and went to sleep.

Mrs Chiffle was a restless sleeper, and every time she turned over the bed went *whump!* and woke Midnite up, so that he had a very bad night. Several times during the night Khat came in, and whispered that there was not a sign of troopers for miles around; but Midnite thought that it was best to stay where he was and trust Mrs Chiffle. At last, towards daybreak, he fell into a sound sleep. He was wakened by Mrs Chiffle, all fresh and smiling, saying: 'Captain Midnite, your breakfast is ready.'

Midnite was very tired and stiff, but Mrs Chiffle cooked the best breakfasts in the Colony, and he soon cheered up again. As he was drinking his coffee, holding up his handkerchief with one hand so that he could get to his mouth, Mrs Chiffle said: 'Captain Midnite, please to write in my Visitors' Book.'

'Your Visitors' Book, ma'am?' said Midnite, surprised.

'My Visitors' Book,' said Mrs Chiffle, putting a large book in front of him, and giving him pen and ink.

So Midnite wrote in the book as follows:

DATE
6/6/66

NAME
Captain
Midnite

ADDRESS
The Secret
Hideout,
W.A.

REMARKS
The underneath
of Mrs Chiffle's
bed is remarkably
free from dust
and fluffy stuff.

When she had read what Midnite had written, Mrs Chiffle smiled, and then blushed, and said: 'Captain Midnite, I have something to confess to you.'

'Yes, ma'am?' said Midnite.

'There were no troopers here last night,' said Mrs Chiffle. 'I told you a story.'

'But why, ma'am?' asked Midnite, wrinkling his forehead.

'It has been my lifelong ambition,' said Mrs Chiffle, 'to hide a bushranger under my bed.'

'Oh,' said Midnite, not very pleased. 'Then I wish you had been satisfied, ma'am, to hide a bushranger under your bed for ten minutes, instead of for ten hours.'

'Forgive me, Captain Midnite,' said Mrs Chiffle.

'I forgive you,' said Midnite, who had enjoyed his breakfast. 'But I am not going to give you back your jam.'

After that, he shook hands politely with Mrs Chiffle, and went off into the bush with his saddlebag full of jam, which he fastened securely to Red Ned's saddle. Then Midnite and Khat sprang on to Red Ned's back, and the Gang dashingly galloped away to the Hidden Valley.

'I really don't understand human beings,' Midnite said to Khat, in a puzzled voice.

'It is true,' said Khat, 'that they are very complicated.'

'But *you* understand them,' said Midnite.

'Oh, *I* understand them,' said Khat, of course. They are not nearly so complicated as cats.'

3

The Queen Versus Midnite

One afternoon when Queen Victoria was playing croquet in the gardens of one of her palaces with the Prince of Wales and the Prime Minister and the Poet Laureate, she suddenly stopped playing and looked thoughtful. It is hard to tell whether she was losing because she was thoughtful, or whether she became thoughtful because she was losing and wanted to change the subject. At any rate, the Queen stopped and said: 'What is the news of Midnite?'

'Nothing new, Mama,' said the Prince of Wales. 'He is ravaging and pillaging the Colony quite as usual.'

The Poet Laureate, who was poetic, began to say something about Robin Hood.

'Stuff and nonsense,' said the Queen. 'There will be no Robin Hoods in Our reign.'

The Prime Minister, a very smooth person, murmured: 'I agree with Her Majesty. This ruffian must be abolished.'

'*Is* he a ruffian?' asked the Prince of Wales. 'He is said by Mrs Chiffle to be most polite.'

'A preposterous woman,' said the Queen, crossly, taking off her crown and mopping her brow with a priceless handkerchief. 'We are hot and disagreeable,' she explained. 'We shall go and sit in the shade.' And she walked away towards a small throne under an immemorial elm tree, taking by surprise the three little maharajahs who held up the train of her robes when she played games, so that they were dragged along behind.

The visitors sat down in the grass and watched as the Queen's giant Nubian slaves fanned her with peacock feathers. When the Queen looked cooler, the Prince of Wales remarked: 'Mama, I think you are unjust to Midnite. He is only young, after all.'

'And he is very romantic,' said the Poet Laureate.

'And you, sir,' said the Queen to the Prince, 'are also young. And you, sir,' she added to the Poet Laureate, 'are also romantic. And for these reasons, Captain Midnite, We suppose, should be forgiven?'

'Ha ha ha,' laughed the Prime Minister, like a waterfall of brilliantine. 'Your Majesty is very quick.'

'Dear Prime Minister,' said the Queen, fondly, 'what is your opinion of Midnite?'

'He is a danger to property, Ma'am,' said the Prime Minister. 'He is a revolutionary. The very money in the Bank of England grows nervous and pale when he is spoken of. Abolish him, Ma'am.'

'So We shall,' said the Queen, with a stern glance. 'Poet Laureate, ring the bell for the Postmaster General. We are going to write a letter.'

The Queen wrote the letter, and the Postmaster General posted it, and it went away on a beautiful sailing ship, called a wool-clipper, in the direction of the Indian Ocean. After many storms and shipwrecks and mutinies and murders of captains by cannibals on desert islands, the ship arrived at the coast of Western Australia, and the one sailor who had not died of scurvy on the voyage ran with all speed to Government House.

The Governor was walking in the garden near the river, wearing a hat with ostrich feathers on it and a gold sword. 'What is it?' he asked the ragged and unhealthy-looking sailor, as he languidly took a pinch of snuff.

'A letter from Her Majesty,' said the sailor, and with a loyal smile he dropped dead.

The Governor read the Queen's letter, and turned pale as he read. This is what it said:

The Tower of London
4th July, 1866

Sir,

It is with feelings of anger and dismay that We read daily in Our loyal *Times* of the liberties taken by horrid Captain Midnite with the people, horses, cattle, sheep and money of Our beloved Colony. It is Our will and pleasure that Midnite be abolished on receipt of Our letter. If this is not done, We shall have no choice but to withdraw Our patronage.

Yours etc.

VICTORIA R.

'Heavens,' groaned the Governor, as he paced back and forth. 'I shall lose my House and my job, and all because of Midnite.'

Just then he saw a long thin smiling man walking towards him. The man stopped and saluted very politely, and the Governor said to himself: 'What a nice-looking chap.'

'Trooper O'Grady, Your Excellency,' said the man, 'at your service.'

'I am delighted to see you,' said the Governor. 'I have just had a threatening letter from the Queen.'

'Oh?' said the trooper. 'How did it leave Her Majesty?'

'Very cross,' said the Governor. 'Her Majesty insists that Midnite be abolished immediately.'

The trooper sucked in his cheeks, and gave a low whistle. 'It will not be easy,' he said, shaking his head.

'It is impossible,' sighed the Governor. 'The man is a demon, a Master Mind. I think you will soon have a new Governor, Trooper O'Grady.'

35

'Your Excellency,' said Trooper O'Grady, with his nicest smile, 'be a man, Sir. Don't give way to despair, Sir. With skill and courage, even Midnite himself can be outwitted.'

'Do you think so?' exclaimed the Governor, eagerly. 'Thank you for those bold words, Trooper O'Grady.'

'Your Excellency,' said the trooper, taking off his hat in an important manner, 'I will swear an oath, here in your presence. Until Midnite is captured, I shall not rest. I will be like the bloodhound, Sir. I will be like the hawk, Sir. That man will be captured, Sir, or my name is not O'Grady.'

The Governor, who did not know that O'Grady's name was really Murphy, cheered up tremendously at this fighting speech, and cried: 'Spoken like a man! Shake hands, O'Grady.'

'Thank you, Sir,' said O'Grady, wringing the Governor's hand most heartily. 'I shall leave today, Sir. You will hear good news from me before long.'

'Good luck and God speed,' said the Governor, shaking hands again. 'The best wishes of the Empire go with you.'

Then O'Grady bowed, and put on his hat, and went away with a firm step to have a glass of beer, leaving the Governor staring at his right hand and wondering what had become of the ring that was usually on it.

One day Midnite sent Gyp to Mrs Chiffle's house to borrow a cup of sugar, and when Gyp came back he had a letter in his collar. Midnite opened it, and this is what he read:

MRS CHIFFLE
Requests the pleasure of
CAPTAIN MIDNITE'S company
AT DINNER
On Friday, the 13th of October,
At 5 o'clock

Midnite had never been out to dinner, and he was rather

curious to know what a dinner-party was like. But at the same time, he saw that it might be dangerous. After talking over the matter with Khat, he wrote the following reply:

CAPTAIN MIDNITE
has much pleasure in accepting
MRS CHIFFLE'S
INVITATION
for October 13th,
but begs to inform
MRS CHIFFLE
that if this is
A TRAP
then CAPTAIN MIDNITE'S
FEROCIOUS SIAMESE
CONFEDERATE
will boil
MRS CHIFFLE
in Oil, and send her Skeleton
to
THE MUSEUM

Midnite gave this letter to Major, who flew away with it to Mrs Chiffle.

When Friday came, Midnite beat his sheepskin shoes with a broom, and put a clean handkerchief over his face, and rode off to the dinner-party. He left Red Ned in the bush, as usual, and crept up to Mrs Chiffle's house. The house was full of lamps and people talking and laughing, and when Midnite peered in, he could see nothing but beautifully dressed ladies. It certainly did not look like a Trap, so Midnite pulled his hat down over his eyes and pulled his handkerchief up to his cheek-bones and went in.

'Dear Captain Midnite,' cried Mrs Chiffle, running to meet him. 'How good of you to come.'

'It is a pleasure, ma'am,' said Midnite, shyly.

37

'Step immediately into the drawing room,' said Mrs Chiffle, 'and be presented to my guests.'

As soon as Midnite walked into the drawing-room, all the visitors went: 'Ooooh!' and Midnite saw that there was nobody there except ladies. Mrs Chiffle was a fairly clever woman, and she knew that although most of the ladies in the Colony were in love with Midnite, most of the men in the Colony wanted to put him in gaol. So she had not invited any men at all.

Midnite stood there looking at the ladies and blushing under his handkerchief, and feeling very shy because he had never spoken to a lady in his life until he had met Mrs Chiffle. As he looked at the ladies, something funny happened to him, and he clutched his chest and groaned.

'Captain Midnite,' said Mrs Chiffle, 'what is the matter?'

'My heart,' groaned Midnite.

'Why,' said Mrs Chiffle, getting worried, 'are you ill?'

'I think I have fallen in love,' said Midnite.

'Oh, how romantic,' exclaimed Mrs Chiffle. 'Who is it? Do tell.'

'No, Mrs Chiffle,' said Midnite, gritting his teeth. 'This secret I must keep locked in my own breast.'

After making this resolution, he walked sternly round the room, shaking hands with the ladies. But when he came to the young lady who had caused him to fall in love, he was so nervous that his hand shook and he dared not look at her.

This young lady was called Miss Laura Wellborn, and she was exceedingly beautiful. I am not going to say what colour her eyes were or what colour her hair was. You will just have to imagine for yourself the most beautiful young lady in the world.

'Why, Captain Midnite,' said Miss Laura, in a voice like music, 'how cold your hand is, and how nervous you are.'

'It is nothing, Miss Wellborn,' said Midnite bravely. 'An old wound that troubles me at this time of the year.'

Then he took Miss Laura's arm and they went in to dinner, and a very good dinner it was, although it was awkward for Midnite to have to push his fork up under his handkerchief, and he got rather messy. As well as good food there was a lot of Mr Macpherson's famous wine, but Midnite did not have any, because he thought it might not be good for him. After dinner they all went back to the drawing-room, and Mrs Chiffle gave Midnite a cigar, but he did not smoke it in case it should make his teeth turn yellow. Then all the ladies fetched their music, and played the piano and sang.

This went on for a long time, and Midnite was getting rather bored; but when Miss Laura Wellborn got up to sing, he felt quite differently. First Miss Laura sang a song which must have been very funny, for all the ladies were laughing, but as it was in Scotch Midnite could not understand a word of it, except for a bit of the chorus, which went:

> Och, Jock, dinna flee!
> What, art thou fear't o' me?
> Bide under my plaid a wee,
> My dowsy gowkit laddie.

Whenever she sang this part, Miss Laura looked at Midnite with smiling eyes, and he got very hot under his handkerchief, although he had never heard a sillier song.

Next, Miss Laura sang a song with a sad yet gay tune, and she sang with her sad, gay eyes fixed on Midnite. This is what the song said:

> 'Alack, alas!' cried Robin Hood,
> 'I am a thief, a thief full bold;
> But Marian is a better thief,
> And steals my heart, as I steal gold.

No better thief lives under sky
Than Beauty in a woman's eye.'
    Hey nonny no!
    Poor Robin Hood!
      Love hunts thee down
      In the green green wood.
    Hey nonny nonny no!
    Hey nickle nackle now!
    Hey needle nardle noo!
    Hey cockadoodle doo!
      Bow wow!

When Miss Laura had come to the end of this beautiful song, Midnite could do nothing except look at her, and Miss Laura suddenly laughed and said in her musical voice: 'I know one thing about Captain Midnite. His eyes are blue.'

'Oh, are they?' said Midnite, blushing.

'Well, of course they are,' said Miss Laura. 'Don't you know what colour your own eyes are?'

That made Midnite extremely miserable, because it showed that Miss Laura thought he was stupid. He *was* stupid, as a matter of fact, but he did not know this, and he did not like Miss Laura to think so.

Soon afterwards he said good-bye to all the ladies and went back into the dark bush where Red Ned and Gyp and Major and Khat were waiting. Then he and Khat sprang into the saddle, and they all galloped away.

It was still spring, and the air smelled of all the flowers in the bush, and the moon was out, and it was such a beautiful night that they went on galloping and galloping for miles and miles and almost forgot where they were going. Midnite was thinking about Miss Laura, and Khat was thinking about whatever it is that cats think about. They must have galloped for half an hour when they came to some fields full of grape-vines and a house with lights in the windows.

'What house is that?' said Midnite to Khat.

'It is Mr Macpherson's cellar,' said Khat, 'where he makes the famous wine.'

'I have never tasted wine,' said Midnite.

'Nor have I,' said Khat.

'I should like to try it, just once,' said Midnite. 'Shall we bushrange some?'

'Why not?' said Khat. 'It is a beautiful night for bushranging.'

They left Red Ned and Gyp and Major in the deep shadow under some olive trees, and stealthily crept up to the house. They could tell by the lights behind the curtains that Mr Macpherson had visitors in the drawing-room, but the end of the house where the cellar was looked dark and safe. There they found a small door, and Midnite boldly forced the lock and led the way down the stairs into the cellar.

The moonlight lit up the whole room, and they saw that it was filled with huge dark barrels lying on their sides.

'Every one of them is full of wine,' whispered Khat.

There were a lot of funny-shaped glasses on a table, and Midnite took one and went to a barrel which had a sort of tap on it, and filled the glass to the brim.

'What is it like?' asked Khat.

'It is hard to describe,' said Midnite, tasting the wine. 'It is rather sweet, and when you swallow it, you feel warm.'

'Let me taste it,' said Khat.

So Midnite searched around until he found a little basin, and filled it with wine, and set it on the floor for Khat.

'It is unusual,' said Khat, when he had tried it.

'Do you like it?' asked Midnite.

'I love it,' said Khat, and he went on lapping up the wine as fast as he could go.

What Midnite and Khat did not remember was that wine and such things have a kind of poison in them, which gets into people's heads and makes them silly, so that they cannot think or talk properly. This is called getting drunk. After

Midnite had swallowed ten glasses of wine, and Khat had lapped up three basinfuls, this is how they were talking.

'I am in love, Khat,' said Midnite, 'with a beautiful angel called Miss Laura Wellborn.'

'That's nothing,' scoffed Khat. 'I have been in love nine times.'

'You are a darn liar,' said Midnite.

'Did you call me a darn liar?' said Khat.

'Yes, I did,' said Midnite.

'If you were not so stupid,' said Khat, 'you would know that it is dangerous to call me a liar.'

'Why?' said Midnite.

'Because I might cut you up in little pieces,' said Khat, 'and post you in a brown-paper parcel to a false address.'

'You do not know how to post a parcel,' said Midnite.

'If you ever call me a liar again,' said Khat, 'I will learn.'

Midnite did not know what to say to that, so he filled his glass and Khat's basin, and they were quiet for a while.

'What does it feel like,' Khat asked, in a more friendly voice, 'being in love with Miss Laura Wellborn?'

'It makes me cry,' said Midnite, bursting into tears.

'Then why be in love with her,' said Khat, 'if it makes such a donkey of you?'

'You have no heart, Khat,' said Midnite, sniffing.

'That is not true,' said Khat. 'I have a heart, and a brain as well.'

'I'm awfully miserable,' said Midnite.

'Why?' asked Khat.

'I think Miss Wellborn thinks I'm stupid.'

'She had better not think that,' said Khat, crossly. 'Nobody is allowed to think you are stupid except me.'

'Thank you, Khat,' said Midnite, stroking Khat's fur. 'You are a good friend.'

'I am the best friend you have, Midnite,' said Khat, purring.

They had another glass and another basin of wine, and then Khat started running around in circles and jumping in the air. 'Wheehee!' he called. 'Look, I can fly. I can fly roun' roun' roun' roun' like Major. You fly too, Midnite.'

Midnite tried to fly, but he was too heavy. ' 'S no good,' he said, laughing. 'Khat, you can't talk properly.'

'You can't talk properly, too,' said Khat.

'Can't I, though?' said Midnite. ' 'S funny.'

' 'S funny,' agreed Khat, giggling.

'Wha's'matter?' asked Midnite.

'You're drunk,' laughed Khat.

'Drunk?' laughed Midnite.

'Wine makes people drunk,' said Khat. 'I forgot.'

'Wine makes cats drunk, too,' said Midnite.

' 'M I drunk?' asked Khat.

'Yes!' cried Midnite, with a shout of laughter, 'You're drunk as a skunk, an' so'm I.'

They laughed and laughed and laughed until they choked on their wine. Then there came a sudden sound at the door that led from the cellar to the house, and they stopped laughing.

'Quick, hide,' whispered Khat, staggering behind a barrel.

But it was too late for Midnite. The door opened, and there stood Mr Macpherson with a lantern.

'Midnite!' exclaimed Mr Macpherson, when he saw Midnite's sheepskin shoes.

'Yesh,' said Midnite, starting to laugh again. 'I'm drunk, Mr 'Phershon.'

'Trooper O'Grady!' called Mr Macpherson, into the house behind him.

'Yesh?' called Trooper O'Grady's voice, coming nearer. 'Wha's'matter?'

'Trooper O'Grady's drunk, too,' giggled Midnite.

'So he ought to be,' said Mr Macpherson, sternly. 'He has drunk six bottles of my famous wine.'

Trooper O'Grady came to the door at the top of the stairs and stood there beside Mr Macpherson, smiling all over his face.

'Hullo, Midnite,' he said. 'How're you?'

'I'm happy,' said Midnite. 'How're you?'

'Come up here,' said Trooper O'Grady. ''S dark down there.'

'All right,' said Midnite, beginning to climb the stairs, and falling all over the place.

'Careful,' said O'Grady, laughing.

'Don't laugh,' said Midnite, laughing too. ''S not funny.'

'What a chap you are,' said O'Grady. 'Here, grab my hand.'

So Midnite grabbed the trooper's hand, and the trooper hauled him up the stairs to the top. By that time they were laughing fit to bust.

'Wha's funny?' asked Midnite.

'You're funny,' said O'Grady.

'I'm not funny,' Midnite said. 'My cat's funny.'

'Why's your cat funny?' asked O'Grady.

'My cat's drunk,' said Midnite.

'What?' said Trooper O'Grady, roaring with laughter. 'What d'you say?'

'My cat's drunk,' said Midnite, laughing in the trooper's face, 'an'-he-can't-talk-properly.'

Then Midnite and Trooper O'Grady hung around each other's necks and laughed and laughed until they were tired, and until O'Grady had picked all Midnite's pockets. After that, O'Grady put the handcuffs on Midnite's wrists, and took him away to the great grey gaol by the sea.

4

Midnite Rides Again

When Midnite woke up the next morning in the prison, he felt as people usually feel after drinking a lot of wine: that is, he felt awful. His head was aching and his mouth tasted like a sheepskin shoe. But soon afterwards Trooper O'Grady brought him a cup of beef tea, and when he had drunk that he seemed to be a little stronger.

'How are you now?' asked the trooper, who looked a bit pale himself.

'Not so bad as I was,' said Midnite, sadly.

'We have to go to the Court today,' said the trooper. 'Here is a glass of rum to give you courage, in case the Judge sentences you to be hanged by the neck until you are dead.'

'I shall never touch Drink again,' said Midnite, in a stern voice.

'I hoped you would say that,' said O'Grady; and he emptied the glass in one swallow.

Midnite got out of bed, and washed his face and cleaned his teeth and combed his hair. 'I wish I did not feel so miserable,' he said.

'Mrs Chiffle has sent you a cake,' said Trooper O'Grady, 'with a file and rope ladder in it, but I am afraid you are not allowed to have presents like that.'

'Never mind,' said Midnite. 'It makes me happy to know that I have a friend.'

'That's the spirit,' said the trooper. 'And you have a better friend in me. Now, hold out your arm to be handcuffed, and let's go to Court.'

Handcuffed together, Midnite and the trooper walked through the great grey echoing corridors of the prison, listening to the prisoners groaning and clanking their chains and shaking the bars of their cages. The huge iron door clanged shut behind them, and they were out in the street of the town. The sun was shining and the wind was blowing off the sea, and all of a sudden Midnite wanted so badly to be free that he almost cried.

As they came towards the Court, Midnite saw a great crowd of ladies waiting outside. That made him nervous, and he hung back and dragged on the handcuffs.

'What's the matter?' asked Trooper O'Grady, stopping.

'I feel shy,' said Midnite.

'Hold my hand,' said the trooper, kindly. So hand in hand they walked through the crowd, and it was not so bad as Midnite had expected. All the ladies stood on tiptoe and stretched their necks to see him, and cried: 'Isn't he handsome! Oh, doesn't he look fierce!' although to tell the truth Midnite was neither fierce nor handsome. But he was young and very strong, and that was enough for the ladies. They wanted him to be handsome, and so that is the way they saw him.

When Midnite and O'Grady came into the Court, which was packed with ladies, all waving fans, they found Judge Pepper sitting on his Bench writing in a book. As soon as the Judge looked up and saw Midnite, his face went purple and he shouted: 'Guilty!'

'Guilty of what, Your Honour?' asked Midnite.

'Guilty of stealing my watch and money,' said the Judge, 'and threatening to tear out my heart and eat it.'

'Excuse me, Your Honour,' said Trooper O'Grady, 'that threat was made by the prisoner's ferocious Siamese confederate, who has never been seen.'

'Whose side are you on?' demanded the Judge.

'Oh, yours, of course,' said the trooper.

'Then keep your evidence to yourself,' snapped the Judge.

At that moment a beautiful bad-tempered cockatoo flew in through a window behind the Bench, and sat down on the Judge's great grey wig.

'What are you staring at?' said the Judge to Midnite.

'You, Your Honour,' said Midnite, grinning.

'Don't be impertinent,' said the Judge, flying into a rage.

If the Judge had ever watched a flock of cockatoos in a tree, he would have known that among cockatoos rage is infectious. But he did not know this; and he did not know, either, that he had a cockatoo sitting on his wig. So without another thought he flew into a rage.

Major's crest shot up like an opened fan, his breast-feathers puffed out, and in half a second he looked twice as big and most remarkably like Judge Pepper.

'Silence in Court!' shouted the Judge, banging on the Bench with his hammer; for the whole Court was laughing.

Major wanted silence just as indignantly as the Judge did, and he furiously flapped one wing as if he wished that he had a good big heavy hammer of his own, and opened and closed his beak very fast as if he were saying rather impatient things about some people.

'Silence!' screamed the Judge. 'If there is any more laughing, this Court will be abolished.'

Major cocked his head on one side and looked suddenly thoughtful. He did not know what all the noisy people were carrying on about, but it occurred to him that if he went to bed, they might be polite enough to stop. So he put the tip of his wing to his beak, as if to say *Sssh!*, and dropped his head on his breast and closed his eyes. Of course, he didn't really go to sleep; but he wanted the Court to be quiet so that he could hear what Judge Pepper had to say before he took action against him.

The plan turned out to be a good plan. The Court was not abolished, and as Major had stopped behaving like a small Judge Pepper sitting on Judge Pepper's head, the laughter raggedly died away. Soon, thanks to Major, there actually was a kind of silence in Court, setting aside a few silly giggles from Trooper O'Grady.

'Prisoner at the Bar,' said the Judge, with a snarl of relief, 'have you anything to say before I pass sentence?'

'Yes,' said Midnite.

'What?' said the Judge.

'Please don't pass sentence,' said Midnite. 'I'm a bush-ranger, Your Honour. I was not made to live in a prison.'

'You should have thought of that,' said the Judge, 'before you stole my watch and money.'

'But I didn't,' said Midnite.

'You didn't?' said the Judge, furiously. 'Why, I gave them to you with my own hands.'

'*He* stole them,' said Midnite, pointing at Trooper O'Grady. 'He picked my pocket.'

Trooper O'Grady suddenly slapped himself on the fore-head, as if to get even with himself for having a bad memory. He put his hand in his pocket and brought out the Judge's watch and purse. 'It is true, Your Honour,' he said. 'I did release them from the prisoner, and in the excite-ment I forgot to give them back to you.'

'Throw them here,' said the Judge suspiciously.

Trooper O'Grady threw the watch and purse to the Judge, and the Judge carefully counted his money. Then he looked fiercely at Trooper O'Grady. 'There are four gold sovereigns missing,' he said.

'*He* took them,' said Trooper O'Grady, pointing at Mid-nite.

'I did not,' said Midnite. 'I didn't have time. *He* took them.'

'Did I?' said Trooper O'Grady. 'Well, perhaps I did. Keep it back from my wages, Your Honour.'

Judge Pepper put his head on one side and stared ferociously at O'Grady. The movement roused Major, who put his head on the other side, and stared ferociously at everybody else.

'Silence in Court!' shouted the Judge, as everyone burst out laughing.

All the noise was making Major quite savage, and he especially did not like to have people shout and bang so loudly when he was sitting on their wigs. So he puffed up all his feathers in a splendiferous rage, and did his best to scream: 'Silence in Court' over and over. His beak and tongue moved so fast that they were just a blur, and his wing battered the Judge's head with an invisible hammer.

'Silence! Silence! Silence!' screamed the Judge. His hammer broke, and he threw the pieces at Trooper O'Grady. 'The prisoner is sentenced to twenty-five years in the great grey gaol.'

'What for?' Midnite shouted back, above the noise.

'For laughing,' shouted the Judge.

'*He* is laughing, too,' shouted Midnite, pointing at Trooper O'Grady, who was laughing so hard that he was bursting his buttons.

'Prisoner at the Bar,' shouted the Judge, 'you will do yourself no kind of good by making preposterous charges against the police.'

'He is my best human friend,' shouted Midnite. 'I want him to be in gaol with me.'

'Out of the question,' shouted the Judge. 'Judges do not send troopers to gaol. If you behave yourself, Trooper O'Grady can come and visit you on Sundays.'

'I don't think I will be in gaol next Sunday,' shouted Midnite.

'What, what, what?' shouted the Judge. 'What's that you say? Not in gaol next Sunday? You will be in gaol for the next one thousand three hundred Sundays. Take him away!'

When the Judge said that, Major shot up his crest, puffed out his feathers, flapped his wings, and with a tremendous shriek flew out of the window clutching the Judge's wig in his claws. It was never found again. Major dropped it in the river, where it was swallowed by a shark, who carried it away inside him to the Red Sea.

Trooper O'Grady and Midnite went back to the great grey gaol handcuffed together, and when they came to Midnite's cell, the trooper took off the handcuffs and said goodbye.

'I will visit you on Sunday,' said O'Grady, shaking hands.

'I don't think I shall be in gaol on Sunday,' said Midnite.

'Well, I will come and see,' said O'Grady, 'and if you are not, I will leave a message.'

Then O'Grady waved his hand, which had the Governor's ring on it, and went away with a regretful face to play billiards, while Midnite sat down on his bed to wait for his supper.

Soon it was dark outside, and the warder came to Midnite's door with the evening meal. First the warder undid the chains that fastened the door, then he undid the three bars across it, then he unlocked the door with a great grinding key, and gave Midnite a knife and fork and some bread and water. After that, the warder locked everything up again, and clipclopped away down the echoing corridors.

Midnite sat down on his bed and ate and drank the bread and water. As he was swallowing the last crumb, he heard a sound on the window sill, and when he looked up he saw Khat peering through the bars.

Khat looked awfully sick. 'Khat, you do look awfully sick,' said Midnite.

'It is the wine,' said Khat, in a tired voice. 'I shall be all right in a day or two.'

'I will never touch Drink again,' said Midnite.

'Nor will I,' said Khat. 'It is a kind of poison.'

'I have had a miserable day,' said Midnite. 'I am in gaol for twenty-five years.'

'Oh no, you're not,' said Khat.

'Are you going to rescue me?' asked Midnite.

'You are going to rescue yourself,' said Khat. 'This is not a very strong cell that you are in, and Major and I have been working on it. If you come here to the window, you will see where we have been digging at one of the bars, which is not very firm in the wall. Go on digging with your knife and fork, and you will be able to pull it out of the wall and wriggle through.'

'Bravo, Khat,' said Midnite, and he started digging away with his knife and fork. Before long, being very strong, he was able to pull the bar right out of the wall. He tied the bar in a knot and left it on his bed, in order to strike terror into the heart of the warder. Then he wriggled through the window and dropped on to the back of Red Ned, who was waiting outside for him.

'Come, Khat,' cried Midnite. 'Come along, Gyp and Major.' And the Gang galloped off into the darkness.

Soon they came to a long new bridge, with a white ribbon across it.

'What is that, Khat?' asked Midnite, as Red Ned broke the ribbon.

'It is to show that the bridge is new,' said Khat. 'The Governor was going to cut the ribbon with some gold scissors and declare it open tomorrow.'

'Oh,' said Midnite. 'Do you think we should be riding on it?'

'No,' said Khat; 'but it is a great honour.' And so they galloped on.

They galloped and galloped all night, and Midnite was so happy to be free again that he cheered and sang all the way. At last the beautiful sunrise shone over the bush, and they found themselves in Midnite's orchard, where the fruit trees were covered in pink-and-white blossom, and the butcher-birds were warbling in the tall forest.

Red Ned was so tired by that time that Midnite decided not to go to the Hidden Valley until the next day. And so, after feeding the animals, he cooked a hearty breakfast for himself; and then, in the room where he had slept ever since he was a little boy, and still listening to the birds in the forest at their morning song, he fell into a deep and happy sleep.

While Midnite was sleeping in the house in the orchard, Dora was taking a thoughtful walk in the bush outside the Hidden Valley. Dora had learned to open and close Midnite's gate, and she often went off for a stroll by herself, to show the other cattle that she was superior. But on this day, Dora was out walking with a special purpose. Midnite and the rest of the Gang had not been home to the Hideout for two nights, and Dora was exceedingly worried about them. So she wandered and wandered, and pondered and pondered, and hoped that somewhere she might find their tracks and be able to follow them.

As she walked through the beautiful, misty, sweet-smelling bush, Dora found that her worries were fading away, and that she grew happier and happier. The reason was that on the very next day Dora was expecting to have a little new calf, and nothing in the world makes a cow so happy and thoughtful and soft-hearted as that.

Presently Dora heard a manly voice singing to itself in the bush, and when she stole up to investigate, she found a tall black horse grazing in a clearing, and a long thin man sitting by a campfire and singing as he watched and waited till his billy boiled.

This is what the man sang:

> A little bit of sugar
> And a little bit of tea,
> A little bit of flour
> You can hardly see,
> And without any meat
> Between you and me:
> It's the murder of a life
> By Christmas.

'Alas,' thought Dora, soft-heartedly, 'it is a poor jolly swagman, who is Down On His Luck. And he is such a nice-looking chap.'

She stood peeping at him from the bush, and wondering whether, when the billy boiled, he might not like some milk for his tea.

Just then, the man began talking to himself. You may have noticed that in real life people do not talk to themselves very much, and you rarely hear them say anything interesting; but it is different in books, and this is a true book. While Dora listened, the man spoke to himself as follows:

'I. WHY DO I WANT TO BE MIDNITE'S BEST HUMAN FRIEND?'

('A friend of Midnite's!' thought Dora, growing excited. 'I shall most certainly offer him milk for his tea.')

The man continued:

'I want to be Midnite's best human friend because he is an idiot. Everybody likes me at first, and says that I am a nice-looking chap. Yet when they know me better' (and here a tear rolled down the man's cheek) 'they say I am a dirty rotten Rogue Cop. But Midnite is so stupid that he will always like me, and will go on thinking me a nice chap for ever after.'

Dora was rather puzzled by this speech, and did not know quite what to make of it. If she had been a more experienced cow, she would have known from the man's clothes that he was not a jolly swagman at all, but a trooper. But Dora had never seen a trooper before, and so she had to wait for the man to explain himself.

The trooper continued:

'2. WHY DO I WANT TO KEEP MIDNITE IN THE GREAT GREY GAOL?'

('*What?*' thought Dora, pricking up her ears. 'Why, this must be the man I have heard them speak of! This must be Trooper O'Grady!' And in a second or two, Dora had changed from a soft-hearted cow to a cow so ferocious that she could hardly keep herself from bellowing like a wild bull.)

O'Grady went on:

'(a) I want to keep Midnite in the great grey gaol because then I shall always know where he is, and it is no use having a best friend if you never know where to find him.

(b) I want to keep Midnite in the great grey gaol because then the Queen and the Governor will be pleased with me, and will give me medals, and will promote me from a pick-pocket to a misappropriator.

(c) I want to keep Midnite in the great grey gaol so that I can continue to do what I am doing today, which is to search for his Secret Hideout in order to bushrange all his plunder.'

That was too much for Dora; and with a thunderous bellow, she came crashing out of the bush, and galumphed across the clearing with her head down and her sharp horns aimed at O'Grady.

54

When O'Grady saw what he thought was a wild yellow bull galumphing towards him, he sprang to his feet uttering one shriek, and ran up a tree with the speed of a lizard. The consequence was that Dora crashed full tilt into the tree trunk, which did not improve her temper at all, and for some minutes she stood there shaking her head and muttering the most terrible mutterings.

It happened that the tree Trooper O'Grady had run up was a very young gum tree, of the kind that bends if you put too much weight on it, and for this reason Trooper O'Grady had not been able to run up it very far. In fact, he had not been able to climb far enough to get his legs out of Dora's reach. As Dora looked at Trooper O'Grady's legs, and Trooper O'Grady looked down over his shoulder at Dora, they both remembered a rather awful story that they had heard from their mothers. This story was about a man who had run up a tree to get away from a bull, and had not been able to get his legs out of range of the bull's tongue. What the bull had done was to lick and lick at the man's legs with his rough tongue until the legs were all licked away.

Dora and Trooper O'Grady considered this story, in their different ways, for several minutes. Then, with a faint blush and a few flicks of her horns, Dora tore off Trooper O'Grady's trousers and began to lick his legs.

Trooper O'Grady gave the most hysterical shriek that has ever been heard from a trooper, and flew to the top of the tree like a bird. But the tree, as I have said, was a springy sort of tree, and with the weight of O'Grady near the crown of it, it began slowly and gracefully to bow towards the ground.

'Jolly good,' thought Dora; and as the tree-top came within her reach, she seized some branches between her teeth and pulled with all her weight. Then, when she had stretched the tree hard and tight, she jumped back and let go.

Like an arrow shot from a bow, Trooper O'Grady sailed across the clearing, and landed in a prickly bush.

'Harrumph!' bellowed Dora, galumphing towards him.

'Help!' shrieked O'Grady. And without a look behind, he sped away, through the lovely early morning bush where all the kookaburras were laughing their heads off.

So great was O'Grady's speed that his horse had quite a job to catch up with him. It was not until he was a mile or more from Dora that the trooper began to feel safe again. Then, after pausing to make a few repairs to himself, he sadly and painfully climbed back in the saddle, and rode off to seek sympathy and trousers.

Two hours later, dressed in a saddle-cloth and with bald patches on his legs where Dora had licked him, O'Grady arrived at Mrs Chiffle's house, intending to ask the good lady whether the late Mr Chiffle had left any unmentionable men's wear behind. What was his astonishment when Mrs Chiffle, at first sight of him, rushed from the house waving her arms above her head in a defiant and exulting manner, and cried: 'Rhubarb to you, Trooper O'Grady! Captain Midnite has Ridden Again!'

5

Midnite's Hairy Godmother

At midday, Midnite rose from his bed in the cottage in the orchard, and set to work to make himself new sheepskin shoes, for his old ones had been forfeited to the Crown, which is a polite way of saying that the Queen had bush-ranged them from him. All afternoon he worked on his shoes, and on soft-soaping his bridle and saddle, and on doing a lot more things that he had been meaning to do before he was put in gaol; and in the evening he lit the lamps and cooked his supper and sat snugly in the kitchen talking to Khat. Khat was feeling much better by then, and even laughed when he remembered how silly Trooper O'Grady had been when he was drunk. While they were talking, they heard a sudden footstep on the verandah.

'Psst!' whispered Khat. 'I am going to hide. Take care.' And he disappeared into another room.

'Who is there?' called Midnite, seizing his pistols and aiming them at the door.

'Only me,' said a funny voice; and the strangest-looking old woman came in. She had an old purple dress, one of those collars round her neck that are made out of a fox, with the eyes still in it, long grey hair like a horse's tail, and a velvet hat covered with flowers and little grapes and bananas and cherries and things that were always nodding and tinkling together.

'Who are you?' said Midnite, sternly.

'A friend,' said the old woman.

'How can you be my friend?' said Midnite. 'I have never seen you before in my life.'

'I am your godmother,' said the old woman.

'Are you, really?' said Midnite. 'I didn't know I had a godmother.'

'Everybody has a godmother,' said the old woman, 'to be kind to them, and cheer them up when they are miserable. That is what godmothers are for, as you would know if you had ever read any fairy-stories.'

'Well, that is a good idea,' said Midnite, 'and I *was* miserable, yesterday, but I am quite happy today, thank you.'

'I shall make you even happier,' said the old woman.

'How?' asked Midnite.

But the old woman only shook her head and smiled. 'You are in too great a hurry,' she scolded, fondly. 'Why, here am I, your godmother, visiting you for the first time, and you have not even asked me to sit down.'

Midnite blushed to think that he had been so bad-mannered, and he quickly led the old woman to his best chair, and begged her to make herself comfortable.

The old woman sat back in the chair in the easiest manner, with the ankle of one leg cocked over the knee of the other, which caused her purple skirt to take on rather a curious shape, and said: 'So *this* is where you live.'

'Yes,' said Midnite, cautiously, for he did not intend to tell his godmother about the Hidden Valley.

'And very nice, too,' said the old woman. 'Are you all alone?'

'Oh, no,' said Midnite. 'I have a Gang.'

'Ah,' said the old woman, looking at him with twinkling black eyes. 'And where are they?'

'Out,' said Midnite, vaguely.

All this time he had been studying his godmother as

closely as he could without seeming to stare at her, and he had come to the conclusion that he was exceedingly glad that she had not kissed him. Although it was obvious that his godmother had quite recently shaved, she had dark bristles all over the lower part of her face, and she looked very prickly. Her hands, too, had black hairs on the backs of them, and from the little that could be seen of her, Midnite judged her to be the most preposterously hairy old woman in the whole Colony.

'Well,' said the old woman, cackling, 'you will know me again, I dare say.'

'I am sorry,' said Midnite, with a blush. 'I did not mean to stare, but you are so extremely different from anybody else.'

'Yes, indeed,' said the old woman. 'I am the only person like me, and you should be proud to have me for your god-mother.'

'Oh, I am,' said Midnite, trying very hard to sound as if he meant it.

The old woman crossed her legs in the opposite direction, settled herself again, and remarked : 'At this hour, I usually have a drink.'

'So do I,' said Midnite. 'I have cocoa.'

'Do you, really?' said the old woman. 'I have a whisky and soda.'

'I am sorry,' said Midnite, 'but there is no whisky in my house, and there never will be.'

'No, no,' said the old woman, with a wave of her hand, 'don't apologize. Cocoa will do very well.'

So Midnite got up and made two cups of cocoa; and when the old woman was seated across the table from him, he said: 'You told me just now you would make me even hap-pier. How?'

'Ah,' said the old woman, 'now we come to it. Well, dear old chap, I am going to sing you a song.'

59

'A song?' said Midnite.

'A song,' said the old woman, 'which will make you pleased and proud. It is a song about a bold bushranger and his name is Midnite.'

'That is very interesting,' said Midnite, laying down his pistols on the table. 'I hope you do not need music or a piano, because I have not got any.'

'No,' said the old woman, 'I make it up as I go along.' And she began to sing, in a preposterous voice:

> ' 'Tis of a wild Colonial boy, Captain Midnite
>   was his name,
>   Of poor but honest parents he was born at—'

Here the old woman stopped, and asked: 'Where were you born?'

'At Blackadder Creek,' said Midnite. 'If you are my godmother, you should know that.'

'Do you mind,' said the old woman, 'if I call it Blackadder *Drain*? Then my song will almost rhyme.'

'You must do what you think best,' said Midnite. 'I don't know the first thing about poetry.'

The old woman started again, and sang this verse:

> ' 'Tis of a wild Colonial boy, Captain Midnite
>   was his name,
>   Of poor but honest parents he was born at
>   Blackadder Drain,
>   He was his father's only hope, his mother's only
>   joy,
>   And dearly did his parents love the wild
>   Colonial boy.'

'That is very nice,' said Midnite, with a tear on his cheek as he thought of his father and mother.

'There is better to come,' said the old woman. And she went on:

'He was scarcely seventeen years of age when he
    left his father's home,
And through Australia's sunny clime a bush-
    ranger did roam.
He robbed those wealthy squatters, their stock
    he did destroy,
And a terror to Australia was the wild Colonial
    boy.'

'Am I, really?' said Midnite. 'A terror to Australia?'

'And to New Zealand,' said the old woman. And she continued:

'In sixty-six this daring youth commenced his
    wild career,
With a heart that knew no danger, no foeman
    did he fear.
He stuck up the country mail-coach, Judge
    Pepper he did annoy,
Who trembling, cold, gave up his gold to the
    wild Colonial boy.'

'That's jolly good,' said Midnite, laughing. 'But don't say
anything about Trooper O'Grady picking my pocket.'

'No, I won't,' promised the old woman; and she went
on:

'He bade the Judge: "Good morning" and told
    him to beware:
For I'd never rob a hearty chap, that acted on
    the square;
But a Judge that would rob a mother of her
    only son and joy
Is no better than an outlaw," said the wild
    Colonial boy.'

'I *didn't* say that,' remarked Midnite.

'Never mind,' said the old woman. 'You forgot to say it.'
And she went on:

> 'One night as he sat in his lair, the mountain-side
>   along,
> A-listening to his godmother, her pleasant
>   laughing song,
> A trooper called O'Grady (well, that name he
>   did employ)—'

'Midnite!' called Khat, from the next room. 'Do you know who this is?'

'Aha!' said the old woman, 'the Siamese confederate.' And she sang in a different voice:

> 'Reached out and snapped the handcuffs on the
>   wild Colonial boy.'

'Shoot, Midnite! Shoot!' called Khat.

'Too late,' said the old woman, drawing a pistol out of her bosom, and sweeping up Midnite's pistols from the table. 'And this time I'll have the Siamese confederate too, or die in the attempt.'

'Then you'd better die now, O'Grady,' called Khat, 'and not tire yourself out for nothing.'

'You're under arrest!' shouted the old woman, rushing into the room that Khat's voice was coming from. But the room was quite empty, and the window was only open about six inches, far too little for even a very small Siamese man to have got through.

'Strange, strange, strange,' muttered the old woman, coming back into the kitchen.

'Are you really O'Grady?' said Midnite, staring at the old woman with his mouth open.

'Yes, indeed,' said the old woman, with a smile that crinkled up her face.

'I don't believe you,' said Midnite.

'I am,' said the old woman. 'Honour bright.'

'Take off your hat,' said Midnite.

The old woman took off her velvet hat with all the

flowers and fruit on it; but she still looked like an old woman with hair like a horse's tail.

'Do you believe me now?' she asked.

'No,' said Midnite. 'Take off your hair.'

The old woman took off her hair and put it on the table, and slowly a smile began to creep across Midnite's face. He looked at the old woman's button-up boots, then he looked from bottom to top of her purple dress, then he looked at her fox-fur collar, and finally he looked at O'Grady's face sticking up out of it. Then he threw back his head and laughed until he was weak.

'What's the matter?' said O'Grady, grinning. 'What's the joke?'

But Midnite could only gurgle and choke.

'No, tell me,' said O'Grady, starting to laugh himself.

Midnite got up from his chair and took O'Grady by the arm and led him to a looking glass. And when O'Grady saw himself, he shouted: 'Oh, good grief!' and went into hysterics.

So Midnite and Trooper O'Grady hung round each other's necks and laughed until they were tired, and until O'Grady had picked all Midnite's pockets. Then O'Grady put the handcuffs on Midnite, and took him away again to the great grey gaol by the sea.

When Midnite and Trooper O'Grady walked to the Court the next morning, there was an even bigger crowd of ladies outside it; but this time Midnite was not so shy, and he waved to them quite sternly. Mrs Chiffle was there, flourishing a flag and cheering, and so was the Governor. Midnite bowed to the Governor, and the Governor took off his hat with the ostrich feathers on it and bowed back. It was lucky that Midnite was holding Trooper O'Grady's hand, or the Governor might have seen that the trooper was wearing his ring.

When Midnite and O'Grady arrived in the Dock, which is a kind of cage for prisoners at the Bar, Judge Pepper was writing in his book. He had made himself not a bad sort of wig out of one of Midnite's sheepskin shoes, but when he looked up and saw Midnite his face went purple and he shouted: 'Villain! Where is my wig?'

'I have no idea,' said Midnite, which was true. 'I never saw it again after it flew out of the window.'

'Lies! Lies! Lies!' shouted the Judge. 'Do you deny that that preposterous cockatoo is a member of your Gang?'

'That has nothing to do with me,' said Midnite. 'If he wants to belong to my Gang, I can't stop him. Have you ever tried to stop a cockatoo from doing anything he wanted to do?'

'Guilty!' shouted the Judge, banging on the Bench with his shoe.

'Guilty of what?' asked Midnite.

'Aiding, abetting, procuring and giggling at the bushranging of my wig,' said the Judge. 'Fifty years in the great grey gaol. Take him away!'

So back went Midnite to the clanking, clanging, groaning, echoing prison, and this time they put him in a much stronger cell, with bars that nobody could tear out of the wall. And when night came, and the warder brought him his supper, he found that they had given him a knife and fork made of wood.

'This is going to be difficult for Khat,' said Midnite to himself, as he sat on his bed staring at the stone slabs of the floor between his feet.

Just then he felt a kind of scratching on the underneath of the stone. He took his wooden knife and fork and dug around the edge of one of the slabs. And when he lifted it, up jumped Gyp, covered with earth, and kissed Midnite all over his face and inside his ears.

'Ah, Gyp, you are a good friend,' said Midnite, kissing him back. Then he wriggled down the tunnel that Gyp had dug, and sprang on to Red Ned's bare back behind Khat, and they galloped away.

6

Miss Laura Wellborn's Adventure

When Midnite came home to the Hidden Valley, with Red
Ned and Major and Gyp and Khat, he found that Dora had
been worrying about them so much that she had got quite
thin and sensible. But she soon cheered up, and was as silly
as ever, and she took Midnite for a ride on her back and pretended to be a wild bucking bull, as she used to do when
Midnite was a little boy. While Midnite was away from the
Valley, she had had a beautiful calf, which staggered when
it walked, and she was offended with Khat for saying that
her baby was drunk.

After they had settled down in the cave again, Khat had a
serious talk with Midnite, and this is what he said.

'We must lie low,' said Khat, 'and give up bushranging
for a while. You are in great danger. There are more troopers
and black trackers looking for you than ever there were
before, and they know about the cottage in the orchard,
and it is possible that the Queen may have bushranged that
from us already. A great many people have seen your
face, including the Governor and Judge Pepper and Trooper
O'Grady. The black trackers know about your sheepskin
shoes, and they may even know Red Ned's hoofmarks. We
must stay in the Valley and never go out or make any fresh
tracks, because if they track us here, then there is no place
in the Colony that is safe for us.'

'That is good advice, Khat,' said Midnite, 'and I think we need a holiday after all this arresting and escaping.'

'Sooner or later,' said Khat, 'we might build a canoe and go bushranging down the river. That way we would leave no tracks, but it would be dangerous if we were seen, because then they would know that our Hideout is on the river.'

'Well, we won't do it yet,' said Midnite, 'but it is an interesting plan, and would be good practice for later on, when I become a pirate.'

'Are you going to become a pirate?' said Khat.

'Some day,' said Midnite. 'However, we shall wait until Dora's calf is grown up.'

Weeks went by without anybody going out of the Valley, except Major, who flew, and left no tracks. They were all feeling quite safe, and rather bored, when one day a startling thing happened.

Midnite was down at the gate, mending a place where the kangaroos had broken it, and whistling at his work, when Major came flying overhead calling his *Danger!* call and wheeling in a great circle round and round something in the bush. As Midnite straightened up and listened, he heard the sound of a horse's hoofs coming towards the gate.

Dropping his tools, he ran for the cave, and seized his gun and lay down behind a rock to watch the gate.

It was not easy to see who was opening the gate, because of the rocks and bushes in the way, but it seemed to him that it was a person dressed all in green. He whispered to Khat, who had crept up beside him: 'Can you see? Who is it? How many people?'

'I can't tell,' said Khat, in a serious voice, narrowing his eyes.

'What shall I do?' asked Midnite.

'You have not done a murder yet,' said Khat. 'This is the time to begin.'

'Must I?' said Midnite.

'You must,' said Khat, sternly. 'I'm sorry.'

By this time the person who had opened the gate had got back into the saddle and was riding towards the caves. As he peered through the rocks and bushes, Midnite made out that it was a person wearing a long green skirt, and riding side-saddle.

'It is a lady,' gasped Midnite.

'So it is,' said Khat, in a wise voice.

'It is Miss Laura Wellborn,' cried Midnite.

'I thought so,' said Khat, more wisely still.

'What shall I do now?' asked Midnite.

'Shoot her,' said Khat.

'Never!' cried Midnite, jumping up and leaving the gun behind the rock. 'I would sooner die.' And he tied his hand-kerchief over his face and pulled down his hat and strode off to meet Miss Laura Wellborn, while Khat slowly and thoughtfully followed.

'Aha, Captain Midnite,' said Miss Laura, as he came up. 'I have tracked you down at last.'

'You have indeed, Miss Wellborn,' said Midnite, 'and I hope you are alone.'

'Quite, quite alone,' said Miss Laura, 'and rather proud of myself, I do assure you.'

'As you well might be, Miss Wellborn,' said Midnite, 'but you have put yourself in an awkward position.'

'Why, Captain Midnite,' said Miss Laura, 'what do you mean?'

'I mean,' said Midnite, 'that I cannot let you go home again, and you will have to stay here in the Secret Hideout for ever after.'

'But how romantic!' cried Miss Laura.

'Do you think so?' said Midnite. 'Truly?'

'Quite delicious,' said Miss Laura. 'I shall be your Maid Marian, and we shall go bushranging together, and we shall be the talk and terror of Australia.'

Midnite was getting very hot under his handkerchief with blushing, and he said: 'Do you mean that you are going to – going to *marry* me, Miss Wellborn?'

'Why, not if it makes you so frightened,' laughed Miss Laura.

'It doesn't make me frightened,' said Midnite, 'it makes me shy.'

'Ah, pure manly heart,' said Miss Laura. 'Now, help me from the saddle, Captain Midnite, and lead me to your dreadful den, and we shall talk about it.'

So Midnite helped her, and took her down, leaning on his trembling arm, to the cave, and gave her his best sheepskin to sit on. And all the time, as she looked round the cave, Miss Laura was saying: 'But how brigand-like! But how exquisitely barbaric!' And all the time, as Miss Laura was saying these things, Khat was looking at her with cold blue eyes.

At last, when Miss Laura had admired everything in the cave and had told Midnite the names of all the painters whose pictures it reminded her of, she said, with a beautiful blush: 'Captain Midnite?'

'Miss Wellborn?' said Midnite, in a rather shaky voice, because he was more in love than ever.

'Would you do something for me?' said Miss Laura.

'I would do anything,' said Midnite, 'anything at all.'

'Then,' said Miss Laura, 'unveil that face, which has been gazed upon by Mrs Chiffle and five hundred other ladies, but has never been gazed upon by me.'

'My face, Miss Wellborn?' said Midnite. 'Do you want to see my face?'

'Captain Midnite,' said Miss Laura, 'I yearn, I crave, I thrill in the anticipation of seeing your face.'

Although Midnite did not always understand the long words that Miss Laura used, he did understand that she wanted to see his face rather a lot. So he took off his hat,

69

and pulled down his handkerchief, and then stood looking at her, expectantly.

Whatever it was that he expected, it was not what Miss Laura did: which was to put her hands over her face and burst into tears.

'Why, Miss Wellborn,' said Midnite, 'what is the matter?'

'You are not handsome at all,' sobbed Miss Laura, 'and your hair needs cutting, and you are only a Boy.'

'I am a young man!' cried Midnite, crossly. 'Look! Feel my face. Whiskers!'

'I hate and despise your preposterous whiskers,' said Miss Laura. 'Take me home immediately to my father.'

'Oh, Khat,' sighed Midnite, whose feelings were so hurt that he was more miserable than he had ever been in his life, 'what shall I do now?'

'Come outside,' whispered Khat, too low for Miss Laura to hear.

So Midnite and Khat went out of the cave, and Khat said to Midnite: 'This is very serious.'

'I know,' said Midnite.

'You cannot take her home,' said Khat. 'She would tell everybody about the Hidden Valley.'

'I know,' said Midnite. 'But what else can I do?'

'Shoot her,' said Khat.

'No,' said Midnite. 'She is too beautiful.'

'Well, then,' said Khat, 'the only thing to do is to keep her prisoner, and perhaps when she is used to us she will be less preposterous. But I doubt it.'

'I shall do my best,' said Midnite, sadly. And he went back into the cave and told Miss Laura that she was a prisoner.

'Is that your last word?' said Miss Laura.

'Yes,' said Midnite.

'You will rue this hour,' said Miss Laura, ferociously. And she did not speak to Midnite again all that day. He tried to be nice to her by showing her his collections of birds' eggs and butterflies and stones, but she only yawned and made a face as if they were disgusting. She made a face at all the things in the cave, which she had admired before, as if they were disgusting; and when Midnite cooked her supper, which Midnite and Khat thought was a very good supper, if not the best supper they had ever seen and tasted, she pushed her plate away and made a face as if *that* was disgusting. But worst of all, when Midnite suggested after supper that she might like to play draughts with him, she made a face as if *he* was disgusting. After that, she took her sheepskin into a corner and lay down and cried all night, in a very loud and public manner.

The next day she decided to start talking again, but that was worse than her silence and her faces, because she went out of her way to hurt everybody's feelings. When she saw Midnite and Dora playing at being a bullfighter and a fierce Spanish bull, she said: 'Master Whatever-your-name-may-be, do you think it wise to excite that ramshackle old cow?' She told Major that his voice was like fingernails scraping on a blackboard. She annoyed Gyp by calling him 'Pup', and asking him if he would like her to scratch his tummy. And she embarrassed Red Ned by knowing the names of all the parts of his body, and finding fault with them.

The only person she was not rude to was Khat. That was because she was clever, and had a plan.

When night came, Miss Laura sat on her sheepskin next to the lantern, and let down all her beautiful hair. She bush-ranged one of Midnite's brand-new hair-brushes, which had never been used (but that did not stop her from making a face as if it was disgusting), and she slowly brushed her hair and sang to herself a beautiful song. She was so pretty, and her hair was so long and lovely, that Khat was fascinated, and he crept up and sat down beside her to watch. Then Miss Laura reached out her hand and began to stroke

Khat, as if she hardly noticed what she was doing, and before long Khat was purring.

After a while, Miss Laura said, almost as if she was talking to herself: 'I think it is very noble-minded of you, who are so clever, to work and plan for such a stupid Boy.'

'He is not exactly stupid,' murmured Khat, 'it is only –'. Then he realized that he had talked to Miss Laura, and he looked very foolish.

But Miss Laura laughed, and went on stroking him. 'I had guessed your secret,' she said. 'What were you going to say?'

'It is only that he was brought up in a forest by his father and five animals,' said Khat, 'and he knows hardly anything about human beings.'

'Well,' said Miss Laura, 'you may call him innocent, but I call him stupid, and I am glad that I have you to talk to.'

From that time on, Khat was always with Miss Laura, and he told her things that he had never told Midnite, such as that he was a prince in his own country. He told her that all Siamese cats were of royal blood. He told her that all cats could talk, if they wanted to, but that they usually only talked to witches, because witches were the only human beings who had anything interesting to say. And every time he told her some new story, Miss Laura clapped her hands and cried: 'Oh, how romantic!' and went on stroking him with great respect.

One day when Midnite was outside the cave and wanted to ask Khat's advice about something, he called for Khat, and Khat did not come. So Midnite went into the cave, and there was Khat sitting in Miss Laura's lap, as usual.

'Miss Wellborn,' said Midnite, sternly, 'I must ask you not to pet my cat when I want him.'

'I cannot think what the Boy means,' said Miss Laura, to no one in particular. 'Khat is being so polite as to entertain me.'

When she said that, Midnite had a funny little pain in his heart. He was jealous of Khat, his best friend.

'I do not know what Mrs Chiffle would think,' he said, 'of a young lady who spends all her time talking to cats.'

'At least he is a gentleman,' said Miss Laura.

'A gentleman!' said Midnite, crossly. 'Why, he's not even British.'

'I would sooner talk to a Siamese prince,' said Miss Laura, 'than to any uncouth youth whatever.'

As soon as he heard her call him an uncouth youth (which is a very rude and hurtful thing to say to a young man of seventeen, and Miss Laura knew this when she said it) Midnite strode out of the cave and threw himself down in the grass and swore the worst swear-word that he knew, which was not very bad, because he had been well brought up. As a matter of fact, he said: 'Darn, darn, darn!' about ninety times. When he was tired of swearing, he just lay in the grass with his eyes shut.

Presently he heard a rustle in the grass, and knew that Khat was sitting beside him; but he only rolled over on his side and turned his back on Khat.

Khat reached out and touched Midnite's cheek with a velvet paw.

'Go away,' said Midnite.

'Midnite,' said Khat sadly, 'we must do something.'

'What?' growled Midnite.

'We must get rid of this lady,' said Khat, 'or she will break up our Gang.'

'That is all very well,' said Midnite, 'but how are we to get rid of her?'

'I don't know,' said Khat. 'If she were not so beautiful, we could tie a rock around her neck and sink her in the river.'

'But she *is* beautiful,' said Midnite.

'I know,' said Khat.

'And I am in love with her,' said Midnite.

'So am I,' said Khat.

'Then I think she will be here for ever after,' said Midnite, 'hurting my feelings more and more.'

'That is out of the question,' said Khat, in a desperate voice. 'We shall have to do something, and the something that we shall have to do is going to give us a lot of trouble.'

'What plan is this?' asked Midnite, nervously.

'We shall have to let her go home,' said Khat, 'and we shall have to leave the Hidden Valley and go somewhere else, because we shall never be safe here again.'

'Where can we go?' asked Midnite. 'I don't know of any other place to live.'

'We could go to the Never Never Desert,' said Khat, 'where all the poets and explorers go to die. There would be no bushranging to do there, but we might find some new rivers or lakes or something, and name them after the Queen, and then she might forgive us for being bushrangers, and we might get gold medals from the Royal Geography Society.'

'That is a good plan, Khat,' cried Midnite, growing excited. 'Come, let us tell Miss Wellborn to go home, and start today for the Never Never Desert.'

'It would not be gentlemanly,' said Khat, 'to tell her to go home, all alone. She might meet a bushranger on the way. No, you must take her to some place where her father can fetch her, and the best place I can think of is the Zamia Creek Hotel.'

'Well, we must be gentlemanly,' said Midnite. And he went into the cave and said to Miss Laura: 'Miss Wellborn, we are going to take a ride together, and then I am going to set you free.'

'That does not surprise me,' said Miss Laura, smiling, 'for I knew I should win in the end.'

Midnite did not quite know what he should say to that, so

he went away and saddled Miss Laura's mare without saying anything.

When Miss Laura came out of the cave, wearing her hard round hat for riding, she was looking rather happy, and she was quite polite to Midnite as he helped her into the saddle, which made him happy too. As they rode out of the Valley and through the bush, which smelled hot and sweet and rather like eucalyptus in the summer weather, Miss Laura even talked to Midnite, and told him about her mother and father and about her friends and about a lot of things that she had never mentioned before. So Midnite began to think that it would have been rather nice to stay with her in the Hidden Valley, if only he could be sure that she would always be in such a good mood.

After a while, Miss Laura asked where they were going, and Midnite told her that he planned to leave her at a rather lonely hotel in the bush, where her father could come for her. Miss Laura thought this a very good plan, and for the rest of the journey, as they walked and cantered through the bush, she talked cheerfully to Midnite and Khat, and admired Red Ned's noble-mindedness and Gyp's cleverness and Major's feathers, and was so nice that they were all quite sorry she was leaving them. At last they came to a clearing in the bush beside a road, and in the clearing was the Zamia Creek Hotel.

'Well, Miss Wellborn,' said Midnite, 'here we must leave you, and I am sorry that we have had to keep you prisoner for so long.'

'Captain Midnite,' said Miss Laura, 'you must not run away and leave me like this. Do, please, for friendship's sake, come into the hotel with me, and let us take a glass of wine and a piece of cake together before we part.'

'I have sworn an oath,' said Midnite, 'never to drink wine again; and anyway, I think it might be dangerous.'

'But the place is so lonely,' said Miss Laura, 'that you

could easily escape into the bush if there was danger. And besides, nobody will know you without your handkerchief over your face. They will think you are my brother.'

'Oh, very well,' said Midnite. And he left Red Ned to graze in the bush, and went on, leading Miss Laura's mare, to the hotel.

It was a long, white, one-storied building, with a veranda all around, and flowers and plants in pots on the veranda: a nice place for the country mail-coaches to stop on a hot summer day.

'Are you coming in, Khat?' asked Miss Laura.

'No,' said Khat, thoughtfully, 'I think I shall wait outside, just in case.' And he hid himself under the verandah, where he could hear what people said in the hotel.

'Why,' said Miss Laura, 'I don't believe Khat trusts me.'

'Please don't think that, Miss Wellborn,' said Midnite. 'We all trust you very much.' Which made Miss Laura laugh to herself in a peculiar manner.

When they were sitting in the cool parlour of the hotel, the landlord came to see what they would like to have, and Miss Laura smiled so sweetly that he was quite confused by her beauty and said that they would have tea, as her brother had sworn an oath never to drink wine again. The landlord laughed, and said that the young gentleman was very wise, but that he was glad that not many young gentlemen swore that oath, or the world would be a hard place for landlords. As the landlord was going away, Miss Laura leaned over the back of her chair and said: 'Oh, and let us have a little seed-cake, if you please.' She touched the landlord's hand with her hand as she spoke, and he looked surprised, and hesitated for a moment before he went out.

Midnite noticed this, and he hardly knew what to think. He did not say anything, at first, but he took his pistol out of his coat and laid it on the table in front of him.

'Goodness,' said Miss Laura, 'whatever is that for?'

'Miss Wellborn,' said Midnite, 'I am not going to say that I don't trust you. But just in case you gave the landlord a note when you touched him then, I am prepared.'

'How suspicious you are,' said Miss Laura, gaily. But she blushed just a trifle.

Midnite kept his eyes on the door, and his hand on his pistol. 'The first trooper who comes in,' he said, 'is a dead man.' But nobody did come in until five minutes later, and then it was only a young Irish maid with the tea things on a tray.

Midnite slid the hand holding his pistol under the table, and watched the maid very carefully, in case she might be Trooper O'Grady in disguise. But she had hardly any whiskers, and she did nothing except set the things out and then go away again.

'Well,' said Miss Laura, cheerfully, as she poured the tea, 'do you feel safe now?'

'I don't know,' said Midnite, still watching the door.

'Come,' said Miss Laura, 'drink your tea, for this is the last meal we shall have together, and it ought to be a pleasant one.'

The cup and saucer were placed before Midnite. Still holding the pistol in his left hand, he lifted the cup.

He drank one sip, and he laughed.

He drank a second sip, and he cried.

He drank a third sip, and he fell fast asleep.

When he woke up, he was back in the great grey gaol by the sea, and Trooper O'Grady was picking his pockets and washing his face with a kind of scent called Eau de Cologne, which is very good for headaches.

7

Midnite the Explorer

When Midnite felt a little better, Trooper O'Grady explained to him that Miss Laura had given the landlord of the Zamia Creek Hotel a note, saying that Midnite was Midnite, and that he had kidnapped her. And so, when the landlord made the tea, he had put a great deal of medicine into it, which had made Midnite go to sleep for hours and hours.

As soon as Midnite heard that Miss Laura had betrayed him, he became so miserable that he would not speak to anybody; not even to Trooper O'Grady, his best human friend.

They walked to the Court, and all the ladies were waiting and cheering, as usual, but Midnite did not wave to them or even look at them, he felt so bitter about ladies. He did not even look at Judge Pepper, when they reached the Dock, although the Judge, as usual, turned an interesting purple colour when he saw them.

'What, what, what?' shouted the Judge. 'You two again?'

'Excuse me, Your Honour,' said Trooper O'Grady, 'but I don't think you ought to say: "You two again?" in that tone of voice, when one of us is a police officer.'

'Evil communications corrupt good manners,' snapped the Judge.

'It's not *my* fault,' said the trooper, 'that whenever you see me I am handcuffed to Midnite.'

'Objection overruled,' said the Judge. 'Enough of these extenuations. Before I pass sentence on the prisoner, are there any charges against him?'

'Yes,' said Trooper O'Grady. 'He is charged with kidnapping Miss Laura Wellborn and making her darn his socks and sew buttons on his shirt.'

'*What?*' cried Midnite.

'His shirt?' cried the Judge. 'Prisoner at the Bar, have you only got one shirt?'

'I have got two shirts,' said Midnite, 'but Miss Wellborn has never sewed any buttons on them, or darned my socks, either. She was a great deal too disagreeable for that. And I did not kidnap her. She came and found me.'

'A likely fabrication,' sneered the Judge.

'Miss Laura Wellborn,' said O'Grady, 'states that she was kidnapped in a desperate and fascinating manner by the prisoner, and chained up in a cave, and that the prisoner made a slave of her, and that he was always trying to kiss her, and that she has never had such a romantic adventure in her whole life.'

'That is not true,' cried Midnite. 'Look at my shirt. It has hardly got a button on it. And my socks are full of holes.'

'Guilty!' roared the Judge. 'Your socks are immaterial and a tissue of lies. You are sentenced to ninety-nine years in the great grey gaol for bushranging a young lady. And let this be a lesson to you if ever you are tempted again.'

'Well,' said Midnite, 'I shall say good-bye, Your Honour, because I don't think that we shall meet again.'

'We had better not,' snarled the Judge, 'or I will sentence you to be hanged by the neck until you are dead. Take him away!'

Trooper O'Grady took Midnite's hand, and for the last time they walked from the Court.

Outside the Court was a sumptuous carriage, in which sat the Governor and his lady. The Governor was very well-dressed in black shoes with gold buckles, white silk stockings, white silk knee-breeches with silver buckles on the legs, a coat with gold leaves and branches all over the front and collar and cuffs, and a black hat trimmed with ostrich feathers. He leaned out of his carriage to raise this preposterous hat to Midnite, and Midnite bowed to him.

'Captain Midnite,' called the Governor, 'I should like to speak to you for a moment.'

'Certainly, Your Excellency,' said Midnite, going to the carriage, and dragging Trooper O'Grady after him by the handcuffs.

'I have had a telegram from Her Majesty,' said the Governor. 'It has come by carrier pigeon from a telegraph office in Java. I think that you should read it.'

Midnite took the telegram, and this is what he read:

FEELINGS OF HORROR AND OUTRAGE EXCLAMATION
MARK LIBERTIES TAKEN BY CAPTAIN MIDNITE WITH OUR
LOYAL AND LADYLIKE SUBJECT MISS LAURA WELLBORN
BEYOND FORGIVENESS STOP IF MIDNITE ESCAPES AGAIN
WE SHALL COME AND GOVERN COLONY OURSELF

VICTORIA R

'It is a very cross telegram,' said Midnite to the Governor.

'Very cross indeed,' said the Governor. 'And that is why we have had built for you a rather special cell, and we hope that you will be comfortable in it for the next ninety-nine years.'

'I do not expect to be there for so long,' said Midnite, 'but thank you for thinking of my comfort.'

'I should not count on escaping this time, if I were you,' said the Governor, smiling. 'In fact, I am ready to make a bet with you. If you do escape, then you have won the bet, and you can stay free.'

'Done,' said Midnite, shaking the Governor's hand. 'I do not approve of making bets, but I will bet with you because you are a gentleman.'

'Thank you,' said the Governor, blushing just a shade. 'And now, good-bye, Captain Midnite. I shall come and visit you one Sunday in about twenty years' time.'

With that, the Governor's sumptuous carriage rattled away, and Midnite and Trooper O'Grady stood waving until it was out of sight.

'Well, Midnite, dear old chap,' said Trooper O'Grady, 'come and see your new cell, and tell me what you think of your chances of winning that bet.'

When Midnite had walked through all the echoing, groaning, clanking, clanging corridors of the gaol and had come to his special cell, his heart sank and for the first time he wondered whether perhaps he really was going to stay in prison for ninety-nine years. The floor was of solid rock, the iron bars were as thick as small trees, and the stone walls were hidden behind great beams of a very hard wood called jarrah, studded with huge iron bolts. Midnite sat down on his bed and stared all around, and he just could not see how Khat was going to rescue him this time.

'I don't think my chances are very good,' he said sadly to O'Grady. 'But I do not despair.'

'That's the spirit,' said the trooper, clapping him on the shoulder. 'And I shall come and see you on Sunday, so you have something to look forward to.'

Then O'Grady went out and locked the door, and barred and chained and bolted and pushed a wardrobe against it, and his footsteps went away down the grey echoing corridors.

When his supper came, Midnite found that by the Governor's orders he was not allowed to have a knife and fork, and he had to eat with his fingers.

Days went by, and he became more and more miserable. That was when he wrote his famous life-story for the newspapers, in which he said that he had been captured three times, and the three causes of his being captured were

Wine, Woman and Song. It was a very sad life-story, and he told all the young men of the Colony that they should learn from his mistakes, and lead pure and manly lives, and never have anything to do with Wine, Woman or Song for as long as they lived.

Of course, in his life-story he did not say anything about his Gang, or about the Hidden Valley. He did not know then whether the Hidden Valley had been discovered or not, and he did not find out until Sunday arrived, and Mrs Chiffle came to visit him.

Mrs Chiffle had got a special hat for the occasion, all covered with dahlias, and she brought Midnite a hamper of marvellous food, which he was glad to have, after the warder had taken all the files and rope ladders out of it. Mrs Chiffle said that she was shocked and surprised by Miss Laura's behaviour, and she hoped that Midnite had not suffered too much.

'Not *too* much,' said Midnite, miserably. 'Tell me, ma'am, what is Miss Wellborn doing now?'

'She stays in her room all day,' said Mrs Chiffle, 'and cries.'

'Why?' wondered Midnite.

'She is ashamed,' said Mrs Chiffle, 'because she betrayed you.'

'Is she, really?' said Midnite, puzzled. Then he asked Mrs Chiffle if Miss Laura had told the troopers about the Hidden Valley.

Mrs Chiffle explained to Midnite that when he was captured at the Zamia Creek Hotel, Miss Laura had been very excited, and that was why she had made up the stories about Midnite kidnapping her and keeping her in chains and trying to kiss her all the time. She had told these stories because she wanted all the ladies in the Colony to think that she had had a very romantic adventure. But afterwards, when she remembered how kind and good-natured Midnite was, and how often she had hurt his feelings with her disagreeableness and long words, she was sorry for what she had said. So when the troopers asked her about the Hidden Valley, she said that she had no idea where it was, as Midnite had always tied a blindfold over her eyes, but that she thought it was south of Zamia Creek. That was quite the wrong direction, and by telling this story Miss Laura had kept the troopers out of the way for nearly a week, in the hope that Midnite would escape.

It cheered Midnite up tremendously to hear that Miss Laura was now telling stories for him instead of against him and although he never told stories himself, he forgave her because she was a young lady. After Mrs Chiffle had left him, he opened his autobiography and crossed out a line which said: '*A false woman is the fearsomest foe of Man.*'

Before long he had another Sunday visitor, which was Trooper O'Grady, shuffling a pack of cards. The trooper had brought Midnite a box of cigars and a small bottle of whisky to go in his hip-pocket; but as Midnite did not drink whisky, because he had sworn an oath, and did not smoke cigars, in case they made his teeth turn yellow, O'Grady drank and smoked all his presents while he was visiting. He also persuaded Midnite to play a card-game for money, which was a thing that Midnite disapproved of; but since he did not want to seem unfriendly, he agreed to play, and in five minutes O'Grady had won all the money that Midnite kept hidden in his socks, for fear of pickpockets, and had taught him to play for IOUs instead. The IOUs were pieces of paper on which Midnite wrote that he would pay Trooper O'Grady such-and-such a sum as soon as he had it. In this way, O'Grady won nearly one million pounds; and when he left, Midnite felt very miserable at the thought of owing his best human friend so much money, which he could never afford to pay. So he swore a new oath, that he would never again play cards for money, and he wrote this in his life-story, beside his other oaths about drinking Drink and going into hotels.

And the time went by, and soon Midnite had been in prison for ten days. He had never in his life expected to spend such a long time in gaol, and he had almost given up hope of being rescued. But one evening, when the warder brought him his supper, he noticed that something crept in through the open door behind the warder, and soon afterwards he saw two red eyes looking at him from a dark corner.

Midnite said to himself: 'What has red eyes when it looks at you from a dark corner?' And he answered himself: 'A Siamese cat!' He was so excited that he almost cheered when he thought this. But he held the cheer in until the warder had gone, and then he let it out, loud and long.

'Hush, my dear Midnite,' said Khat; but he said it fondly, because he was very pleased indeed to see Midnite again. 'There is a plan afoot, and we have not a minute to lose.'

'Oh, good for you, Khat,' cried Midnite. 'I was afraid I really should be here for ninety-nine years.'

'You ought to have had more faith in me,' said Khat, sternly. 'Now, there are two jobs for you to do. First, look out of the window and tell me if you see anything interesting in the sky.'

Midnite looked out between the bars, and after a while he said: 'There is something that looks like a burning stick flying through the air.'

'Good,' said Khat. 'It is Major, and our plan is going well. Next, wrap yourself up in your blanket and crawl under the bed.'

'Why?' asked Midnite.

'Don't ask questions,' cried Khat. 'Quick! We are in danger.'

So Midnite wrapped himself up and crawled under the bed, and when he and Khat were lying there in the dark, he said: 'Now tell me the plan.'

'It is a long story,' said Khat, 'but the short of it is that Major has been building a nest between the walls of your cell.'

'Why should Major build a nest?' asked Midnite. 'Major is a boy – isn't he? He is not going to lay an egg – is he?'

'I shall take no notice of your stupider questions,' said Khat. 'As you know, cockatoos usually build their nests of grass and leaves and stuff, which is not hard. But this nest of Major's is very big and peculiar and different, and that is why we have been so long in rescuing you.'

'Well, if his nest is not made of grass and leaves and stuff,' said Midnite, 'what *is* it made of?'

'Gunpowder,' said Khat.

Just then something went KER-BOOOOM! and the outside wall of the cell blew up.

After the rocks and beams had finished falling, Midnite and Khat dug their way out from under the bed, and ran through a huge hole in the wall to where Red Ned and Gyp and Major were waiting.

'Bravo, Major!' cried Midnite, as he and Khat sprang on to Red Ned's back. Then they all galloped away together through the dark dark bush.

When they had galloped for miles and miles and had come to the hills, Midnite said to Khat: 'I don't think we need ride so hard, because the Governor has made a bet with me that if I escaped this time, I could go free for ever after.'

'Do you trust the Governor?' asked Khat.

'Yes, of course,' said Midnite. 'He is a gentleman.'

'He is a Public gentleman,' said Khat, 'and Public gentlemen are the last people in the world that you should trust.'

'I think you are unkind, Khat,' said Midnite.

'I think I am sensible,' said Khat. And as it turned out, so he was. For the Governor had got nervous, and had told the police that if Midnite escaped again they were to recapture him at any cost; and when the sun rose among the hills who should Midnite see but O'Grady, riding at the head of a party of troopers.

'Hullo, Midnite!' called O'Grady, spurring his horse forward. 'Wait a bit!'

'No fear,' said Midnite, laughing. And he galloped away as fast as Red Ned could go.

Midnite was a very, very good rider, and at first he quite enjoyed the chase in the fresh morning air. As he raced along, he listened to the warbling butcher-birds and the laughing kookaburras in the bush, and looked at the lovely sunrise that was turning the tips of the gum-leaves pink on all the hills, and he thought to himself how preposterously splendid it was to be a free man on such a day. But Red Ned was tired after coming all the way from the gaol, and the troopers' horses were fresh, and before long they were hardly the length of a cricket pitch behind Midnite.

'Surrender, Midnite,' called O'Grady. 'We are ten to one.'

But Midnite only laughed, and sang over his shoulder, at the top of his voice: ' "I'll fight but never surrender", said the wild Colonial boy.'

'I will shoot your hat off,' shouted O'Grady.

'Try,' laughed Midnite.

As he spoke, a bullet went through his hat. But the hat did not fall off, and O'Grady said a bad word.

'I will shoot it off this time,' swore O'Grady. A second bullet went through the hat, and it spun to the ground.

'Never mind, I shall have another hat in one minute,' called Midnite. And he was right. One minute was all the time it took for Major to swoop down on O'Grady and bushrange his hat, and drop it on Midnite's head as Red Ned sped along.

'You can have my hat now,' offered Midnite. 'I'm sorry it has got bullet-holes in it.'

O'Grady said a very bad word that Midnite had never

heard before, but he did not shoot at Midnite's hat again, because it was his hat and he hoped to get it back.

'Midnite,' said Khat, from the saddle in front of Midnite, 'they are coming awfully close.'

'You can't win, Midnite,' shouted O'Grady. 'We are going to head you off and take you back to gaol.'

'Red Ned, Red Ned,' cried Midnite, looking back at the galloping troopers, 'unless you save me, I may be hanged by the neck until I am dead.'

The words were hardly out of his mouth when O'Grady's horse shot ahead of Red Ned and wheeled to cut him off. But Red Ned swerved to the right; and calling up all his strength and all his noble-mindedness, he raced towards the brink of a narrow ravine.

'Midnite,' cried Trooper O'Grady, 'come back! You will fall into the ravine and be killed, and I couldn't bear it.'

'Red Ned, be careful,' whispered Midnite, who was very worried.

'Midnite,' sobbed Trooper O'Grady, 'don't be killed! You are my only friend, Midnite, and what shall I do without you?'

'Red Ned,' whispered Midnite, patting Red Ned's neck, 'I trust you.' And at that moment Red Ned reached the brink of the ravine, and gathered all his muscles together in one tremendous leap, and sailed like a bird through the empty air to land safe on the other side.

When Midnite looked back, all the troopers had pulled up at the edge of the ravine, and were looking nervously into the emptiness below. All the troopers, that is, except O'Grady, who was clapping and cheering, he was so glad that Midnite was safe, and so proud of him.

Midnite raised Trooper O'Grady's hat politely to Trooper O'Grady, and waved and rode away.

And ever since that day, the place at the edge of the ravine has been called Midnite's Leap. But I think it ought to be

called Red Ned's Leap. After all, it was Red Ned who did the leaping.

When Midnite's Gang reached the Hidden Valley at last, they were all very tired. Midnite and Khat were tired from riding, and Red Ned was tired from galloping and leaping, and Major was tired from flying and from being blown up in the explosion at the gaol, which had gone off sooner than he expected. But the tiredest one of all was poor Gyp, who could not leap or fly across ravines like Red Ned and Major and had had to go right down to the bottom and then come up again, after running nearly all the way from the prison.

Dora had been terribly worried about them, for they had not been home for twelve days, and when she saw Midnite she was so pleased that she galumphed up and kissed him all over with her rough tongue, and wanted to play bullfighters straightaway. But Midnite was so weary that he went into the cave and lay on his sheepskin and fell asleep, hardly noticing the thunderstorm that was going on outside.

When he woke up, late in the afternoon, Khat said: 'We have had a stroke of luck. There has been heavy rain, and if we have left any tracks, they are washed away now. We are safe for a little while.'

'Do you think we can stay here?' asked Midnite.

'No, I don't,' said Khat. 'And by the way, what do you think of the Governor now? You won your bet, and he sent the troopers after you.'

'I have sworn an oath,' said Midnite, sadly, 'never to make bets again.'

'Good,' said Khat. 'And if you do make another bet, watch out for people like the Governor. There is a name for people like that, and if you meet him again, you should tell him that he is a dirty rotten Welsher.'

'I could not say that to a Public gentleman,' said Midnite; 'but I shall remember the name.'

'It is good to live and learn,' said Khat. 'And now, let us talk of more serious matters.'

Then Khat told Midnite his plan. He said that they must leave the Hidden Valley that very night, in case the trackers should find their way there or Miss Laura Wellborn should betray them, and set out for the Never Never Desert. They should take another horse besides Red Ned, to be their pack-horse, and Midnite should make sheepskin boots for the horses, so that they would leave no tracks. And Midnite himself, Khat said, should put on a disguise, to look as much as possible like an explorer, if anyone should ask who he was.

All that afternoon Midnite worked at making the sheep-skin boots for the horses, and at making himself a beard out of the curly ends of cows' tails. When it was finished and glued on, he looked much older, and very like an explorer, and Khat said that he was funny but almost handsome. As soon as it was dark, Midnite's Gang ate their last meal in the Secret Hideout, and said good-bye most affectionately to Dora and her calf, and rode away for they did not know how long through the gate of the Hidden Valley.

For four hours they travelled through the hills and the forest, and then they camped for the night and slept till dawn. When the sun rose, the butcher-birds and the kooka-burras woke them, and they breakfasted quickly round the campfire and set out again on their journey.

It would take a long time to describe all the things that happened to them on this journey, which lasted for a thou-sand miles and led them to places no one had ever seen be-fore. I will describe it as quickly as I can. For the first few days they travelled through grassy plains with trees scat-tered here and there, where there were many crows and cockatoos flying about, and where sometimes they saw cattle and sheep. Then the grass plains gave way to a rather dry country, with very red earth covered with grey-green scrub, and in the scrub they saw a great many kangaroos and emus leaping and bustling along. Sometimes in the soft red dust they saw the tracks of bare human feet, and now and again, out of the corners of their eyes, they would see a movement as a black man hid behind a bush and stared at them. For as long as they travelled, a thousand miles, the black people followed and hid and peeped at them; but Midnite and his Gang never saw a black person, except out of the corners of their eyes.

After about a week, they left the scrub and came to a country where nothing grew on the red stony ground except a kind of prickly grass called spinifex. This was very hard country for them to travel in, because there was scarcely any water, and they would certainly have died of thirst if it had not been for Major and Gyp. But always, just when they thought that they would have to camp for the night without water, Major came flying back calling that he had found some. Sometimes it was only a damp patch in the soil, and in that case Gyp dug a small well for them, as the wild dogs do. Once it was only a few little trees, and they did not know what Major meant until Gyp began digging, and they found water inside the roots. But sometimes it was a rock pool, with pigeons and duck and wallabies around it, and sometimes it was a creek or a small river, and sometimes it was a salt lake. Whenever Midnite found a river or a creek or a lake, he named it after Queen Victoria, and made a note in his Diary.

Presently the stony desert gave way to the most ferocious country anyone has ever seen. It was all soft red sandhills, running east and west, and as the horses struggled to the top of one dune, all they could see ahead of them was more sand stretching for hundreds of miles. There was scarcely even any spinifex there, and the black people got tired and went away for a while and stopped peeping at Midnite, and water was very hard to find. Red Ned and the other horse were often so thirsty that they were quite weak, and everybody was hungry, though Khat and Gyp went out hunting and brought back birds and wallabies and lizards. The only thing that there was plenty of in the Never Never Desert was flies, and they crawled into everyone's eyes, and Midnite's eyes got sore and swelled up; so he called some hills he could see in the distance the Bung Eye Ranges, and made a note in his Diary.

One day when they were travelling through this dreadful country, which had nothing living in it except swarms of flies and green budgerigars, they came to the top of a sand-hill and saw tracks going away and away over the sand ahead of them. 'Hurrah.' cried Midnite. 'It is another ex-plorer, and he has camels.' And they made haste to catch up with the explorer, because they were all feeling rather lost and lonely.

When at last they overtook the explorer, he did not look at all pleased to see them, and he said to Midnite: '*Ach, du lieber*, what do you here without your Papa?' This explorer was a rather miserable German man called Johann Ludwig Ulrich von Leichardt zu Voss, but in Australia he had called himself Mr Smith, and his two bad-tempered camels were called Sturm and Drang. While Mr Smith was talking to Midnite, Sturm and Drang made faces at Red Ned and the other horse, and spat at them, for no reason whatever.

'I am exploring,' said Midnite, feeling shy that he looked so young. I forgot to mention that his beard had fallen off after one day, because the glue had melted in the heat. 'May I ask, where are you going?'

'I too am exploring,' said Mr Smith. 'I am exploring me.'

'How can you explore you?' asked Midnite.

'I will not explain,' said Mr Smith. 'You would have to be me to understand.'

'Well,' said Midnite, blushing, 'I am sorry if I seem stupid.

But at least you won't mind, will you, if I ride along with you?'

'I can you not prevent,' said Mr Smith. 'The desert belongs to everyone.'

'I think you are mistaken,' said Midnite. 'The desert belongs to Queen Victoria, and I have named it after her, and made a note in my Diary.'

The explorer laughed a hollow laugh, and handed Midnite his own Diary, in which Midnite read: *Today have I this desert the Cosmic Symbolical Desert named.*

'I do not like that name half so much as mine,' said Midnite, politely, 'and I see by the date that you named it three days after I did, so I think I shall stick to the name I gave it.'

'You are a free creature, do what you please,' said the explorer, with his miserable laugh. 'You may yourself through the head shoot, I shall not offended be.'

By this time Midnite and Khat had decided that they did not like Mr Smith at all, but they stayed with him for company, as he and Sturm and Drang were the only living things in the desert apart from themselves and the flies. So they travelled with him all day, and in the evening they came down from the sandhills to a white salt lake which was all surrounded by bones.

Midnite stared at the bones with great surprise. He saw horse bones and camel bones and pieces of harness, and boots and belts and hats and blankets, and many many smiling human skulls.

'What is this place?' asked Midnite, in a nervous voice.

'It is the end of Outback,' said the explorer, 'where come poets and explorers to die.'

As he spoke, Sturm and Drang knelt down among the bones, and Mr Smith got off Sturm's back, and the two camels rolled over and expired.

'Why do they die?' asked Midnite, more nervously still.

'Because they themselves exploring finished have,' said the explorer. Then he shouted something in German, and fell down in the bones, dead and smiling.

Midnite and Khat were very sad, even though they had not liked Mr Smith, and they buried him and wrote his name in pencil on a flat stone. Then Khat went out hunting and got some good ducks, and they camped by the salt lake and had supper.

When it was dark, and Midnite lay wrapped in his blanket near the camp fire, he listened to the mournful crying of the wild dogs in the distance, and thought that it was the miserablest place in the whole world. He slept between Gyp and Khat, and he hugged them close to him, he was so glad that they were there. He had almost fallen asleep, when a wind came blowing along the lake and through the bones, and the bones began to sing.

All the bones were singing, all around the lake, so many different songs and poems that he could not hear the words of any poem except one. This is what the bones that were closest to him sang as the wind blew through them:

> 'Out on the wastes of the Never Never –
>   That's where the dead men lie.
> There where the bunyips dance for ever –
>   That's where the dead men lie.
> That's where the Empire's sons are keeping
> Endless tryst; nor the lubras sweeping
> Feverish bullroarers wake their sleeping –
>   Out where the dead men lie.'

'Khat, I'm scared,' whispered Midnite, hiding his head in his blanket.

'So am I,' said Khat; and he and Gyp crawled into the blanket too.

And the bones went on singing:

> 'Home Sweet Homeward their white skulls turning –
>   That's how the dead men lie.

Arm-bones stretched in unarticulated yearning –
    That's how the dead men lie.
Oft when the coolibahs are wagging
Hearing again their mothers' nagging,
Overtook by a dreadful sagging –
    That's how the dead men lie.'

Then the wind died down, and the voices faded, and at last Midnite fell asleep.

When he woke at sunrise, he was so eager to get away from the dreadful lake that he did not stop to have breakfast or clean his teeth or anything. He just rolled up his blanket and started off northward across the desert, which had turned to stony ground and wild red rocky hills, for by then they had left the sandhills behind them.

All day they travelled, and in the late afternoon Major flew over them calling a call that meant that he had found something special. They followed his shadow on the ground and came to a narrow passage in a range of hills, between two vast walls of dark red rock, like the walls of a giant's gaol. They tramped down this passage, hearing every sound that they made echo back and forth between the cliffs, and came out into a place like a paddock among the boulders, in which was a long deep pool, with water-lilies and ducks floating on it, and grass and trees all around it, and a great many comfortable caves.

'Oh, bravo, Major!' cried Midnite, throwing Trooper O'Grady's hat in the air. 'It is another Hidden Valley, and even better.'

Then he and Gyp dived into the pool and had a swim. And when Midnite was cool, he began to gather a few stones together for a fireplace, so that he could boil his billy and make tea.

'That's funny,' said Midnite, as he lifted a yellowish stone. 'This rock is awfully heavy.'

Khat glanced at the stone, and opened his eyes wide, and looked again. 'Midnite,' he said, after a moment.

'Yes?' said Midnite.

'It is gold, Midnite,' said Khat, in a solemn voice. 'You are going to be a millionaire.'

8

Mr Daybrake, Millionaire

The next day Midnite began exploring for gold very thoroughly, and with the help of Gyp he dug up a gold reef running for about a mile under the ground. He put piles of stone around it, to show that it was his, and then he wrote a letter to the Governor. In the letter he said that he claimed the reef for himself, but that anyone was welcome to come and look for gold nearby. He signed the letter P. DAYBRAKE, and gave it to Major to carry to a small settlement on the coast two hundred miles away, where ships sometimes called with beer for the settlers.

When Major arrived at the settlement, a sailing ship was lying at anchor there, and Major gave Midnite's letter and a penny for the stamp to the captain, who was most astonished. The ship sailed away, and before long the Governor was reading Midnite's letter, and throwing his preposterous hat in the air and cheering. The Governor dashed off dispatches to the Queen and the newspapers telling them about Mr Daybrake's reef; and in no more than two weeks' time another ship arrived at the settlement on the coast, with a most extraordinary crowd of passengers. There were Englishmen and Irishmen and Scotchmen and Chinamen and Afghans and Americans, and they poured off the ship and made with all speed for Mr Daybrake's reef, riding horses and camels and donkeys and mules, or walking and running and pushing wheelbarrows and perambulators. Within a week, there was a settlement of tents at Daybrake's Reward, as Midnite's reef was being called. Within a month, there was quite a big town, with five shops and thirteen hotels and a bathroom. They named the town Daybrake, and they elected Midnite its first Mayor.

As soon as Midnite had made his first million pounds, he wanted to send it to Trooper O'Grady, for he was worried about all the money that he had lost to O'Grady at cards. But Khat said that if Trooper O'Grady ever guessed that Mr Daybrake was Midnite, he would find some way to bush-range Midnite's gold and put him in gaol. So Midnite was unhappy in his conscience, and it was very irritating to him to be so rich and not to be able to send presents to Mrs Chiffle or Trooper O'Grady, or to Miss Laura Wellborn, with whom he was still very much in love.

That was when he began to boil his billy with five-pound notes, and to shoe Red Ned with gold.

At the end of his first year at Daybrake, Midnite had three million pounds, and he built a fine house with stained-glass windows and crystal handles on the doors. At the end of his second year, he had eight million pounds, and he built the Daybrake Town Hall for himself to be Mayor in. At the end of the third year, he had eighteen million pounds, and he built the Daybrake Opera House, and invited a famous actress called the Guernsey Rose to come and sing in it. The Guernsey Rose sent him a picture of herself, and said that she was sorry that she was too busy to come, but that she hoped to see him some day in London.

That set Midnite thinking.

By this time, Daybrake was the richest town in the Colony, with wide streets lined with pepper trees, and a Library and a Town Hall and an Opera House, and they were talking of having gas lamps in the streets and a horse-drawn tram. And Midnite was quite definitely the richest man in

the Southern Hemisphere, and all the ladies were in love with him. But they never saw him. There were no ladies at Daybrake, except for a few black ones, who were very shy.

At the end of his third year at Daybrake, Midnite was twenty years old. He had grown rather tall, and very strong, and although he was no cleverer than he had ever been, he was just as good-natured. He still had a brown smiling face and bright blue eyes, and one day, after he had happened to have a haircut, Khat remarked: 'You will be surprised to know that you are *almost* handsome.'

This pleased Midnite very much, and made him think again about Miss Laura, and about the Guernsey Rose, who had said that she hoped to see him in London.

'Shall we go to London,' he said to Khat, 'and spend some of our money?'

'Yes, let's,' said Khat, 'and on the way, I should like to stop at Siam and visit my relations.'

So Midnite put his money in the Daybrake Bank, except for a couple of million pounds which he kept to spend on the journey, and he and Khat and Red Ned and Gyp and Major went to the coast, and took a ship to Siam.

The King of Siam was very pleased to see His Worship the Mayor of Daybrake, and entertained him most politely, and Khat stayed for a few days with his relations in the Cat Palace. But Khat was not happy there. His relations treated him in a rather superior manner, and said that he was rowdy and had got a Colonial accent. So after a week, Midnite's Gang took another ship and went to London.

When the ship arrived at the Tower of London, there was a red carpet on the wharf for Midnite to walk on, and the managers of all the most priceless London hotels were there, begging Midnite to come and stay with them. But Midnite told them that he had sworn an oath never to go into a hotel again, and he stayed instead at a respectable mansion called the YMCA.

Every night Midnite went to the theatre, and after the theatre he had supper with the Guernsey Rose, who was exceedingly beautiful, though not so beautiful as Miss Laura. Every day he and Red Ned went for a canter in the Park, and the ladies passing in their carriages leaned out and peered through their gold binoculars and cried: 'Who, but *who*, is that handsome horse, and that almost handsome young gentleman?' All over the Kingdom, Midnite's Gang was a huge success. Major had his portrait painted sitting on the finger of a Duchess, and Khat had his portrait painted sitting on the shoulder of a witch. Red Ned, who was ambitious in a quiet and noble-minded fashion, won the Grand National and the Derby, and Gyp won all the sheepdog trials in Scotland. And Midnite's great triumph came one morning when he opened an interesting-looking letter and read this:

The Crystal Palace
6th May, 1870

Dear Mr Daybrake,

We have some friends coming to take tea with Us tomorrow. Will you give Us the pleasure of your company also? We hope you will not disappoint Us.

VICTORIA R.

The next day Midnite presented himself at the Palace, dressed in a new tartan suit from Bond Street, and was shown into the Queen's drawing-room by a priceless butler.

The Queen was sitting on her throne at the top of some carpeted stairs, with her long robes trailing down before her. At her left hand was a tall black Zulu king, who was brushing the flies off her with a lion's tail. At her right hand stood a well-dressed Knight of Malta.

'Take these baubles,' said the Queen, giving her orb and

sceptre to the Knight of Malta. Then she rose, and progressed in a majestic manner down the stairs, and held out her hand to Midnite.

'Mr Daybrake?' said the Queen.

'Your Majesty,' said Midnite, bowing low over the Queen's hand.

'Let Us take tea,' said the Queen; and she led the way to the tea table, where two distinguished gentlemen were standing behind their gold chairs and bowing.

'Mr Daybrake,' proclaimed the Queen, 'allow Us to present to you the Poet Laureate, who greatly admires your romantic spirit, and the Chancellor of the Exchequer, who looks after Our money, and of course is most interested in millionaires.'

Midnite bowed to the two gentlemen, and after helping the Queen into her chair, he sat down at her right hand and watched her pour the tea.

'Tell Us,' commanded the Queen, when she had said Grace, 'something of yourself, Mr Daybrake. Who, for example, are your People?'

'My People, Ma'am?' said Midnite.

'Your family, Mr Daybrake,' said the Queen.

'Why, Ma'am,' said Midnite, 'there is very little to tell. My father was a well-born Irish pirate, who hid-out in Madagascar, and retired from the sea to a forest in Western Australia, where I grew up and still have a property, I hope.'

'Indeed?' murmured the Queen. 'We fancy that We have heard your father most warmly spoken of by Her Majesty the late Queen Ranavalona.'

'My mother,' continued Midnite, 'came from a good Colonial family, which arrived in the *Parmelia*. They were of the true old Swan River pioneering breed, and spent their first winter in the Colony camped on a beach underneath their grand piano.'

'What a stirring tale,' breathed the Poet Laureate, scribbling notes on his shirt cuff for a poem.

But the Queen had been looking very thoughtful ever since Midnite had said that his father was a pirate.

'Our cousin, the late Queen Elizabeth,' she remarked, after swallowing a piece of crumpet, 'was in the habit of encouraging pirates, and even of making them Knights. We are not sure that this was the correct idea.'

'Excuse me, Your Majesty,' said the Chancellor of the Exchequer, 'but it was a very good idea from the Exchequer's point of view. The Queen always got her share of the plunder.'

'Money, money, money,' sighed the Queen. 'What was it that you said about money, Poet Laureate, in your rousing poem?'

'This, Ma'am,' said the Poet Laureate; and he thunderously recited:

'ON THE OPENING OF THE EXHIBITION OF ANGLO-SAXON MILLIONAIRES (1869)

> Money to right of them,
> Money to left of them,
> Money in front of them
> – Borrowed or plundered?
> Where did they get the stuff?
> Had they played clean or rough?
> When would they have enough?
> – So we all wondered.
>
> Who could compare with them?
> O! to be there with them,
> A millionaire with them.
> Grabbing one's share with them,
> Swapping the Chair with them,
> Smogging the air with them,
> Renting the fair with them,
> Losing one's hair with them,
> Gobbling *éclairs* with them. . . .'

'That is jolly good, Poet Laureate,' interrupted the Chancellor of the Exchequer. 'Don't you think so, Your Worship?'

'It is a fine, thunderous poem,' said Midnite, 'and very polite to millionaires.'

'Thank you, sir,' said the Poet Laureate, bowing.

The Queen frowned a little, and stared at her plate as she toyed with a piece of cake. 'To return to the subject of pirates,' she said, 'it was surely wrong of Queen Elizabeth to encourage them. Why, it is just as if We were to encourage bushrangers.'

As she said this, the Queen raised her large blue eyes to Midnite's face, and kept them there.

Midnite felt a blush creeping up his face, and could not think what to say.

'And bushranging,' continued the Queen, with her eyes still on him, 'is a kind of stealing.'

'I had not thought of that,' muttered Midnite, blushing red as fire. And he swore a silent oath never ever to be a bushranger again.

'Well, well,' said the Queen, looking him up and down, and at last dropping her eyes, 'what is past, is past. How old are you, Captain – We mean, *Mister* Daybrake?'

'Twenty, Ma'am,' faltered Midnite.

'And how much money have you?' asked the Queen.

'About seventeen million pounds, Ma'am,' said Midnite.

'Chancellor of the Exchequer,' said the Queen, 'what do you think?'

'Excellent, Ma'am,' said the Chancellor. 'Most suitable.'

'Very well, then,' said the Queen, preparing to rise from her chair. 'Mr Daybrake, when you are twenty-one, We think We shall make you a Knight. A Colonial Knight,' the Queen added, 'to begin with.'

'Why thank you, Ma'am,' gasped Midnite.

'It is nothing,' said the Queen. 'Pray, do not think of mentioning it. Richness must be encouraged.'

With these words, the Queen gave Midnite her hand, and he bowed over it and withdrew from the drawing-room backwards, while the Queen slowly mounted the stairs to her throne.

At the top of the stairs, the Queen turned, and called: 'Mr Daybrake.'

'Yes, Ma'am?' called Midnite, from the other end of the drawing-room.

'We think,' said the Queen, 'that perhaps you had better marry Miss Laura Wellborn.'

'Oh, certainly, Ma'am,' gasped Midnite.

'And not,' said the Queen, sternly, 'the Guernsey Rose.'

'Oh no, Ma'am, of course not,' cried Midnite, who had never had any such idea.

'What a very tidy tale it is,' remarked the Queen; and with a weary wave of her hand she dismissed him, and reached for her orb and sceptre.

Midnite was so dazed and excited that he ran all the way from the Palace to the YMCA, and when he got there he panted out to Khat: 'The Queen knows I am Midnite, and she forgives me, and she is going to make me a Knight.'

'Extraordinary,' murmured Khat, in great surprise. 'I did not know that the Secret Service was so clever.'

'Let's go home, Khat,' cried Midnite. 'I am going to gather up all my money, and take it to Miss Wellborn, and ask her to marry me.'

'Marry you?' said Khat, doubtfully. But then he remembered how soft Miss Laura's hand was when she stroked him and how nice it was to sit in her lap, and it seemed not such a bad idea. 'Oh, all right,' said Khat.

The next day, after saying good-bye to the Guernsey Rose, Midnite's Gang went on board a splendid sailing ship; and following a long and adventurous voyage, they arrived at the coast of Western Australia, two hundred miles from Daybrake.

As soon as he reached Daybrake, Midnite bought a coach from Cobb & Co., and painted MR DAYBRAKE, MILLIONAIRE in gold letters on the doors, and loaded into it the sixteen million pounds that he had left behind in the Daybrake Bank. He put Khat and Gyp and Major inside the coach to guard the money; and then, with Red Ned ambling alongside, drove off behind his fine team of horses towards the south and Miss Laura Wellborn.

It would take many pages to describe Midnite's journey, and all the terrible country that he passed through, and all the times that he nearly died of thirst and nearly got speared by black people and nearly got bogged for ever after in the sand. After a month of great hardships, he reached the hills where he had grown up, and had come quite near his cottage in the forest, when a voice called from the bush: 'Stand and deliver!'

'It is a bushranger,' whispered Khat; and he and Gyp and Major jumped quickly out of the coach windows and hid.

Midnite reached for his pistol; but he had no sooner raised it than a bullet knocked it out of his hand.

'You haven't a chance,' said the voice. 'Get down from the box and stand in the road with your hands up.'

Midnite was very unwilling to be shot dead when he had come so close to Miss Laura. So he thought it best to do what the voice told him.

'That's a good chap,' said the voice, which seemed to be laughing. Then a long thin bushranger, with a handkerchief over his face, came out of the bush and poked Midnite in a friendly way with his pistol.

'You don't understand,' said Midnite, to the bushranger.

'What don't I understand?' asked the bushranger, who appeared to be laughing a great deal underneath his handkerchief.

'You don't understand who I am,' said Midnite.

'Well, who are you?' asked the bushranger.

'I'll whisper it to you,' said Midnite.

'All right,' said the bushranger, bending his head.

So Midnite whispered into the bushranger's ear: 'I am a famous bushranger. I am Captain Midnite.'

The bushranger was laughing so hard that he could scarcely stand up, though he still kept his finger on the trigger of his pistol.

'Will you stop that stupid giggling,' said Midnite, crossly.

'I want to tell *you* a secret,' gasped the bushranger. 'May I whisper?'

'All right,' said Midnite, in a stern voice.

The bushranger put his arm around Midnite, and whispered: 'I am Trooper O'Grady.'

'*What?*' cried Midnite, starting back.

'I really am,' laughed O'Grady. 'Honour bright.'

'It's not fair,' said Midnite, with tears of bitterness in his eyes. 'I have worked very hard for three years to get all this money, and now you are going to bushrange it from me.'

'Such is life,' said O'Grady, which was a famous saying amongst bushrangers. 'And to show you what a good friend I am, here is your purse, which I bushranged from your pocket while I was whispering to you.'

'You can keep the darn thing,' said Midnite, furiously. 'I don't want it.'

'Don't you, really?' said O'Grady, dropping the purse in his coat. 'Well, every little helps. Welcome home, Midnite, dear old chap, and it's good to see you looking so fit.'

With these words, O'Grady clapped Midnite cheerfully on the shoulder, sprang to the driver's seat of the coach, and rattled away with Midnite's sixteen million pounds.

9

Miss Laura's Visitors

If Midnite had been less strong and more clever, he might have given way to despair after losing all his money, and done something silly, like joining the Army. But after shedding a few tears, which even a young man of twenty may be pardoned for shedding when it is a question of money, he leaped on to Red Ned's bare back (for even his saddle had been carried off in the coach) and rode away to the cottage in the orchard.

When he arrived there, he found that the orchard had grown very wild and jungly, and that there was a piece of paper nailed to the door. This had once said: MIDNITE'S PROPERTY IS FORFEITED TO THE CROWN, but the words had been crossed out, and underneath, in red pencil, Midnite read: WELCOME HOME BY ORDER OF THE QUEEN. (Signed) THE GOVERNOR.

'So you see,' said Khat, 'it has done you good to be a millionaire for a while, even if you are not one now.'

'That is all very well,' said Midnite, sulkily, 'but it will not do me much good with Miss Wellborn.'

'I think it would be better,' said Khat, 'if she married you while you are poor, for then you can be sure that she loves you.'

'But I wanted her to see me when I was rich,' said Midnite. 'She won't even look at me now. Even my London clothes have been bushranged by O'Grady.'

'You must not talk,' said Khat, 'in this bitter and despairing manner. You may be a millionaire again. You have a reef of gold and a fine hideous house at Daybrake. So long as you have these, you have Prospects. I do not know exactly what Prospects are, but Miss Laura's father will ask you if you have any, and you will be able to say "Yes". So cheer up, and set to work cleaning this cottage, for it is not fit for a cat of royal blood to live in.'

So Midnite swept the house, and pruned and weeded the orchard, and then he and his Gang rode off to the Hidden Valley to find Dora. Just how delighted Dora was to see them, after an absence of three years, it would hardly be possible to describe. It is enough to tell you that Midnite, to please her, rode her all the way home to the cottage, and that he was very stiff afterwards. He was just as pleased as she was, and most surprised to see her calf, who had grown into a grumpy great bull and looked old enough to be her father.

After they had settled in at the cottage, Midnite sent Major with a note to Mrs Chiffle, asking if he could come to tea with her, and explaining that she need not worry about troopers any more, because he had stopped being a bushranger and was a friend of the Queen. Mrs Chiffle wrote back a happy note saying: 'Come tomorrow.'

The next day, Midnite rode up to Mrs Chiffle's front door and Mrs Chiffle ran out exclaiming how nice it must be for him to be respectable, and not to have to hide his horse in the bush or creep into houses wearing sheepskin shoes. It made Midnite a bit sad to remember the exciting times that were past, but he agreed with Mrs Chiffle that it was a good thing to be respectable, and they had tea, and talked about the old days when Midnite was a wild Colonial boy. At last Midnite said: 'And how is Miss Wellborn?'

'Ah,' said Mrs Chiffle, with a shake of her head, 'poor Laura has never been well since you went away.'

'Not well?' said Midnite, 'I'm most awfully sorry to hear that.'

'She has been so sad,' said Mrs Chiffle. 'She is quite pale and faded.'

'I wonder why?' murmured Midnite.

'You wicked Captain Midnite,' smiled Mrs Chiffle. 'You know you have stolen her heart.'

'*I* stolen her heart?' said Midnite. 'But she can't abide me.'

Mrs Chiffle laughed and laughed. 'So Laura may pretend,' she said, 'but I am a lady, and I know better.'

'I am astonished,' said Midnite, with his mouth open. 'But I am glad to know this. It may make things easier for me when I ask her to marry me.'

'Oh, you are going to propose,' cried Mrs Chiffle, clapping her hands. 'How perfect. You must let me help you, you positively cannot do without me.'

'Why, ma'am,' said Midnite, 'I should be pleased to have a lady's advice on this sort of deal, which is rather out of my way. How shall I begin?'

'First,' said Mrs Chiffle, 'give her presents. Little presents, fruit and flowers and things of no value. Then, perhaps, one present just valuable enough to make her take notice. And then you must speak.'

'And say,' said Midnite, 'what?'

'That you love her,' said Mrs Chiffle. 'Be strong. She will refuse you, but be strong. If she faints, ignore her. Say: "Enough of your young lady's nonsense." Sweep her off her feet, Captain Midnite. Do not take "No" for an answer, for she certainly won't want you to. It will all be over in a minute, if you are only strong.'

'It sounds, ma'am,' said Midnite, 'remarkably like breaking a horse, which comes easily enough to me.'

'That is exactly how it should be,' said Mrs Chiffle. 'And now, go to her, with my blessing.'

Midnite rode away from Mrs Chiffle's with a very thoughtful face, and some quite new thoughts behind it.

Miss Laura Wellborn came of an old Colonial family, which had spent its first winter in the Colony camped on a beach inside a china cabinet. Her father was a squatter (that is, he kept a lot of cattle and sheep) and he lived in a big old farmhouse called a homestead. It was a pleasant house, with a pleasant garden, and a pleasant avenue in front of it, where Miss Laura liked to walk.

One day as she was walking in the avenue, she was surprised to see a yellow cow galumphing towards her. On coming nearer, she saw that the cow had a garland of daisies around her horns. The cow came up to Miss Laura, and bowed her head, and Miss Laura took the garland and hung it around her own neck. She said: 'Thank you' to the cow, and the cow bowed again and galumphed away, looking rather silly and not half so young as she thought she was.

'How odd,' said Miss Laura to herself.

The next day, as she was walking in the avenue, a sheep-dog came trotting up to her with a little basket full of strawberries in his mouth, and laid it down at her feet. He looked up at her for a moment with a face that was half laughing and half worried, as if he were not sure whether he had done the right thing. Then Miss Laura said: 'Thank you', and the dog bowed and trotted away.

'Odder and odder,' said Miss Laura, as she took the strawberries to the kitchen.

The next day, as she walked in the avenue, a tall and noble-minded horse came prancing to meet her, with two baskets slung by a strap across his back. One basket was filled with oranges and lemons, and the other with roses. Miss Laura lifted down the baskets, and said: 'Thank you' to the horse, and the horse bowed and pranced away. As he went, Miss Laura noticed that his shoes were of pure shining gold.

'Most exceedingly odd,' said Miss Laura.

The next day, as she walked in the avenue, a cockatoo flew down from a tree and wheeled around her head. 'Come, sit on my hand,' called Miss Laura, stretching her white arm. But the cockatoo swooped close to her hair, and flew off. And when Miss Laura put her hand to her throat, she found that she was wearing a gold chain, which had certainly not been there before.

'This is becoming preposterous,' said Miss Laura, who was beginning to guess.

The next day, as she walked in the avenue, a handsome and superior Siamese cat came stalking to meet her with a long-legged stride. The cat bowed, and said: 'I hope I see you well, Miss Wellborn.'

'How dare your master send me presents,' said Miss Laura in an offended tone.

Khat smiled a little at the idea of anybody being *his* master, and said: 'It is the correct thing, Miss Wellborn.'

'The correct thing,' said Miss Laura, 'when?'

'When he is courting you,' said Khat. 'He is going to ask you to marry him tomorrow.'

'I am surprised that he has the impertinence,' said Miss Laura.

'He is surprised, too,' said Khat. 'It is my impertinence, actually.'

'Then return to him,' said Miss Laura, 'and tell him that I would sooner die than marry him.'

'But why?' asked Khat. 'He is very good-natured, and strong, and not a bit clever.'

'*I* don't want a stupid husband,' said Miss Laura.

'Don't you?' said Khat. 'Most ladies do. He would give

you no trouble, and would always do exactly as you told him. He is also extremely rich.'

'Is he?' said Miss Laura.

'He is rich under another name,' said Khat, 'which you have often heard.'

'Not Mr Daybrake?' cried Miss Laura.

'That is the name,' said Khat. 'And the Queen is going to make him a Knight. Just think: if you were Lady Daybrake, with a rich, stupid, good-natured and almost handsome husband, every lady in the world would be jealous of you.'

'That is true,' said Miss Laura, thoughtfully.

'So,' said Khat, 'shall I tell him that you would sooner die?'

'No,' murmured Miss Laura. 'No. I shall decide tomorrow.'

Then Khat bowed, and said: 'Your servant, Miss Wellborn,' and stalked away. And Miss Laura went to her room, and wrote a long long letter to Mrs Chiffle.

The next day, as she walked in the avenue, she saw a whole party coming to meet her. In the air was a cockatoo with sunrise-coloured feathers; on the road was a laughing sheepdog, and an old yellow cow, and a tall strawberry horse; in the horse's saddle sat a blue-eyed cat, and a blue-eyed long-legged young man.

Midnite had sold Red Ned's shoes and bought new clothes to come courting Miss Laura. He wore high shiny riding-boots, white trousers, a blue coat with silver buttons, and a white hat. As he came near Miss Laura, he swept off his hat and bowed.

'You have had your hair cut,' said Miss Laura, 'finally.'

She said this in a funny voice. She hardly knew what to think of Midnite. She had remembered him as he was when he and she were seventeen; and what she saw now was a young man who could have had a beard if he had wanted one, and was almost handsome.

Midnite slipped from the saddle and stood tall and straight in front of Miss Laura, holding his hat in his hands, and blushing. He cleared his throat as if he were going to say something, but he said nothing at all. At last Khat leaned out of the saddle where he was sitting, and whispered in Midnite's ear.

'I hope I see you well, Miss Wellborn,' said Midnite, suddenly.

'Quite well,' said Miss Laura, looking crossly at Khat.

Khat whispered to Midnite again.

'Miss Wellborn,' said Midnite, 'Miss Laura – may I call you Miss Laura?'

'After the liberties that you have taken with my liberty,' said Miss Laura, going red and speaking only to Khat, 'you may take what liberties you like with my name.'

Khat looked very pleased as he leaned over once more and whispered to Midnite.

'Miss Laura,' said Midnite, 'let me take the final liberty, and take away your liberty and your name both together.'

'I do not know how matters may be arranged in Siamese Cat Palaces,' said Miss Laura, looking furiously at Khat, 'but that is not my idea of being married.'

'Darn!' swore Midnite, throwing his new hat bad-temperedly on the ground. 'It's no use! Miss Laura, I cannot talk like a lady, or a cat. I came here to ask you one question. Whatever your answer may be, there are only two things that I have it in mind to do. One is to marry you. The other is to go back to Daybrake and never see you again. But either way, Miss Laura, I do not mean to put up with any of your disagreeableness, or any of your long words, or any of your darn nonsense whatever. Now, Miss Laura, will you marry me?'

'Oh yes,' said Miss Laura, in a very small voice, as she gazed at him. 'Oh yes, yes, yes, darling Midnite.'

After that, I suppose Midnite kissed her. At any rate, he

did something to her that made a letter slip from her hand and fall to the ground, where Khat read it. This is what it said:

My dearest Laura,
   Play with him! Let him feel your power! ! Make him wait ! ! !
He will respect you all the more in the end.

Ever your most affectionate
EUPHEMIA CHIFFLE

10

What Happened Ever After

On his twenty-first bithday, Midnite was married to Miss Laura. It was a very grand wedding, attended by the Governor and his lady and Mr Justice and Mrs Pepper, besides a great many troopers and warders and other old friends. Mrs Chiffle was there, naturally, as a sort of bridesmaid. And of course Midnite had to have a Best Man, to cheer him up if he got frightened, and of course for his Best Man he chose Trooper O'Grady, his best human friend. It was just as well that O'Grady was there, for when Midnite saw Miss Laura coming up the aisle to marry him, his heart gave a jump and he went weak in the legs and groaned. But O'Grady held him up, and patted him on the back, and said: 'Bear up, old chap,' and he felt better.

Anyone might have gone weak in the legs at the sight of Miss Laura as she walked up the aisle on her father's arm. She was all in white, and her hair was full of orange-blossom from Midnite's orchard, and in her hand she carried a branch of pear-blossom, on which sat Major, as beautiful as any flower. The long white train of her dress was held up by Gyp and Khat, and Mrs Chiffle, in purple velvet and ostrich feathers, walked behind.

When Miss Laura had taken her place beside Midnite, scattering the sweet smell of orange-blossom from her hair, the clergyman opened his book and married them, with

great speed and skill. There was just one happening that ought not to have happened, and I mention it because it should be a warning to all young bridegrooms who have friends like O'Grady not to choose them for their Best Men. Midnite had given the wedding ring to O'Grady to keep in his pocket until the moment came to put it on Miss Laura's finger; and when that moment arrived, it was discovered that O'Grady had seventy-three other rings in his pocket, and it took them five minutes to pick out Midnite's. That was the second time that O'Grady disgraced himself. Only a little while before, when Midnite (who of course used his real name at his wedding) said: 'I, Percival, take thee, Laura,' Trooper O'Grady had giggled in Church. But when they went into the vestry to write in the book, it came out that O'Grady's real name was Ignatius Loyola Murphy, so Midnite had the last laugh.

Or perhaps Khat had it. While they were in the vestry, O'Grady trod on Khat's tail, and Khat said: 'I should watch my feet if I were you, O'Grady, or some day you may find man-eating piranha fish in your bath.' O'Grady looked preposterously astonished for a moment, then he cried: 'Good grief, the ferocious Siamese confederate!' and hit himself on the head with his fist. After that, O'Grady tried to make friends with Khat, and asked if Khat thought of going bushranging again. But Khat had spoken his last word to O'Grady. He knew that they had too much in common ever to be good friends.

Soon all the guests drove away in carriages to Miss Laura's father's homestead, where there was a banquet of splendid food, cooked under the orders of Mrs Chiffle, and gallons of Mr Macpherson's famous wine, which everyone except Midnite greatly enjoyed. Midnite did not drink any. Apart from his oath, he was already drunk on Miss Laura's orange-blossom. Everybody made speeches, especially Miss Laura's father and the Governor and Judge Pepper, and everyone cried a lot, especially Miss Laura's mother and her aunts and Mrs Chiffle. But the one who made the best speech and cried the most was Trooper O'Grady. Tears were pouring down his cheeks as he said that a wedding was a very joyful occasion, and that the two things that made the world go round were Love and Mateship, and that if ever he had had a mate for whom he would willingly die, that mate was Midnite. Then he sang a noble-minded song, which went like this:

> 'Yes ! let me like a soldier fall,
>   Upon some open plain,
> This breast expanding for the ball,
>   To blot out ev'ry stain.
> Brave manly hearts confer my doom,
>   That gentler ones may tell,
> Howe'er forgot, unknown my tomb,
>   I like a soldier fell:
> Howe'er forgot, unknown my tomb,
>   I like a soldier fell,
>   I like a soldier fell.'

Midnite was made pleased and proud by this speech, and he shook O'Grady heartily by the hand and patted him on the back to cheer him up. But he left O'Grady very miserable, and blowing his nose on a new silk handkerchief which he absent-mindedly bushranged from Midnite's breast-pocket.

After saying good-bye to the guests, Midnite took Miss Laura on his arm and helped her into a small carriage, drawn by Red Ned, who looked very fine in a harness covered with shiny brass. Then everyone waved, and Miss Laura threw her branch of pear-blossom to Mrs Chiffle, who screamed as she caught it, and O'Grady mournfully knocked Midnite's hat off with an elastic-sided boot, and the bridal couple clip-clopped away, with Dora galumphing ahead and clanking her best cow-bell.

When they arrived at the house in the orchard, Dora and

Gyp and Khat and Major were waiting on the verandah for them, and Khat said: 'Midnite, before you carry Miss Laura over the doorstep into the house, we have a present for you.'

'Why, thank you, Khat,' said Midnite.

'It is Major's present, really,' said Khat. 'He is the one who bushranged it.'

'Oh, no!' cried Midnite. 'Have you forgotten? I have sworn an oath never to bushrange anything again.'

'But my darling Midnite,' said Miss Laura, 'Major has not sworn an oath.'

'It is very wrong,' said Midnite. 'It is almost like stealing.'

'You will hurt Major's feelings,' said Miss Laura. 'Come, Major, fly to me, and show me the present.'

She held out her arm, and Major flew down and laid his present in her hand.

'What is it, Laura?' asked Midnite.

'It is a great big key,' said Miss Laura, in a puzzled voice. Then she suddenly said: 'Oh!' and laughed.

'The key of what?' asked Midnite.

'It is a present to you,' laughed Miss Laura, 'for your twenty-first birthday. It is the key of the great grey gaol by the sea.'

'Oh, good grief, Major!' cried Midnite. 'You will have us all put in gaol! We must give it back. No, better still, we must give it to Trooper O'Grady. He will need it, sooner or later.'

'That would not be polite to Major,' said Miss Laura. And she hung the key on the gold chain that Major had put round her neck, before she was married, and hid it in her dress. 'I shall keep it,' said Miss Laura, thoughtfully, 'just in case.'

Then Midnite carried her over the doorstep into the house and when they were inside he said: 'Laura, we shall have to go to Daybrake, because I am very poor, and you may not like it there, it is so hot and there are so many flies, and no ladies to talk to except black ones, who are very shy.'

'I shall like it,' said Miss Laura, 'because you will be there. But you must promise always to do what I tell you, and to have your hair cut when I say, and visit the dentist, and change your shirt, and buy new underclothes, and go to Church, and wash behind your ears, and not have friends like O'Grady, and eat your crusts, and wipe your boots, and always come home at exactly the same hour, so that I shall know when to be in an agreeable mood – '

'Such is Life,' cried Midnite, which was a famous saying amongst bushrangers.

'God bless us all,' said Khat.

Then Midnite kissed Miss Laura long and lovingly, and Captain Midnite's Gang lived happily ever after.

HEARD ABOUT THE PUFFIN CLUB?

.... it's a way of finding out more about Puffin Books and authors
of winning prizes (in competitions), sharing jokes, a secret code,
and perhaps seeing your name in print! When you join you get
a copy of our magazine, *Puffinalia*, sent to you four times a year,
a badge and a membership book.
For details of subscription and an application form,
send a stamped addressed envelope to:

The Australian Puffin Club
Penguin Books Australia Limited
P.O. Box 257
Ringwood
Victoria 3134

and if you live in England, for a copy of *Puffin Post* please write to

The Puffin Club Dept A
Penguin Books Limited
Bath Road
Harmondsworth
Middlesex UB7 ODA

Colin Thiele

The Hammerhead Light

To Tessa Noble and the people of Snapper Bay the
Hammerhead light was more than a lighthouse.
It was a symbol of all that was strong and enduring
and safe.

Tessa, growing up within sight and sound of the
Hammerhead, forms a deep bond with old Axel
Jorgenson, the lighthouse keeper. Then both their
lives are changed by a strange migratory bird, the
whimbrel, and Tessa learns the meaning of change
and the pain of growing up.

Magpie Island

Magpie loved the wind and the steep, open sky over
the Eyre Peninsula, which he roamed with his
companions. One day a wedge-tailed eagle came
sailing out of the Nullarbor. Unable to resist
following the eagle, Magpie is seized by the strong
north wind and blown far out to sea. When,
eventually, he lands it is on a gaunt, windswept,
solitary island, and Magpie finds himself among
thousands of strange sea birds . . .

Carol Drinkwater

The Haunted School

Fanny Crowe – kind teacher or wicked witch?
That was the question that troubled unhappy
twelve-year-old Richard Blackburn. For how could
the newly arrived English governess befriend his
sisters by day, yet by night live in the haunted old
building that had caused his mother's tragic death?

It troubled the others, too, for in colonial
Australia superstitions ran strong and the locals
resented an outsider meddling with a past that was
best forgotten. And then there was the loathsome
old hermit from the mountain who had his own
reasons for wanting the new schoolteacher out of
the way . . .

A.B. Facey

A Fortunate Life

Bert Facey saw himself as an ordinary man, but his remarkable story reveals an extraordinary life.

Brought up by his grandmother in the rough West Australian outback, his childhood ended when he was eight. He was forced to go out to work – clearing, ploughing, fencing and droving. By the time he was fourteen he was an experienced bushman, and by eighteen a professional boxer in Micky Flynn's famous boxing troupe.

Bert Facey was a battler, ever optimistic and hopeful despite the hardships in his life.

A classic in Australian writing, *A Fortunate Life* has now been specially adapted for Puffin readers.

Victor Kelleher

The Green Piper

After a mysterious flash of light in the night sky, strange music drifts from the woodland.

To begin with the soft haunting melody entices only birds and animals. But then, three of the townsfolk – Angie, Ross and Mad Jack – are affected.

Alone, unaided, they investigate. And what they discover is both bewildering and sinister.

Papio

It seems simple enough to David and Jem to release the two baboons from the experimental research station where they are doomed to die. But when they discover the baboons are no longer capable of looking after themselves in the African bush, David and Jem are forced to stay and protect them. And that's when their problems really begin . . .

Robin Klein

Hating Alison Ashley

Erica Yorken knew she was destined for a glittering career on the stage. Never in any doubt about her own genius, she felt superior to everyone at notorious Barringa East . . .

That is, until Alison Ashley unexpected turned up.

Alison was not only beautiful, rich and clever, but she was as well-behaved as a nativity angel.

Yet Erica wasn't going to give up that easily and the annual school camp would be the ideal place to show Alison Ashley!

People Might Hear You

'Our religion is for every day we live, every living moment. You musn't ever raise your voice or call out . . . people outside might hear you . . .'

When her aunt marries the forbidding Mr Tyrell, Frances is introduced to the mysterious temple, with its strange, fanatical beliefs. At first she trustingly accepts her aunt's new life, and tries to be a 'worthy' member of the temple. But as she uncovers its sinister secrets she realizes she has to escape.

Kerry Kenihan

Red and the Heron Street Gang

Red lives on the wrong side of town. Whenever people call her Regina she knows she's in trouble and somehow that often seems to happen, especially when she forms a gang to defend her street from the tough Cherry-av kids.

The Heron Street Gang get out of most of their scrapes until one day the Murray River swells into flood, bringing real danger.

Dianne Bates

Piggy Moss

At school they called her a pig, and at home it wasn't much better. There was nobody around, nothing to do, and no one in whom to confide.

When Jack arrived from England, Vivian found a friend and it looked as though her troubles were over. But then came the night of the fire, the terrible family row, her sister's accident . . . and Vivian began to wonder how her family would survive.